I0632725

TEMPUS FUGITIVE

MISSION 1

BLACK OCEAN: PASSAGE OF TIME

J.S. MORIN

Copyright © 2022 J.S. Morin

All rights reserved. No part of this publication may be reproduced, distributed or transmitted in any form or by any means, including photocopying, recording, or other electronic or mechanical methods, without the prior written permission of the publisher, except in the case of brief quotations embodied in critical reviews and certain other noncommercial uses permitted by copyright law. For permission requests, write to the publisher, addressed "Attention: Permissions Coordinator," at the address below.

Magical Scrivener Press
www.magicalscrivener.com

Publisher's Note: This is a work of fiction. Names, characters, places, and incidents are a product of the author's imagination. Locales and public names are sometimes used for atmospheric purposes. Any resemblance to actual people, living or dead, or to businesses, companies, events, institutions, or locales is completely coincidental.

Ordering Information: Special discounts are available on quantity purchases by corporations, associations, and others. For details, contact the publisher at the address above.

J.S. Morin — First Edition

ISBN: 978-1-64355-563-8

Printed in the United States of America

TEMPUS FUGITIVE

MISSION 1

Jessie Ramsey was out of uniform. She had on her flight jacket with Earth Navy insignia, mainly so the Martian customs didn't hassle her over the blaster in her luggage. The rest of her attire was strictly civilian, and she felt like a tourist wearing it. Checking her datapad for directions didn't help.

This was Jessie's first time in New Shanghai, despite dozens of trips to Mars. It bustled like any core world city but had that distinctive "Earth but better" arrogance that bled into the signage, advertisements, and demeanor of the residents.

No one hassled her, which was a welcome relief. Shore leave in Class Cs was one thing. Even the least patriotic ARGO citizens were unlikely to rough up an Earth Navy lieutenant. Or hit on one. Or blow off one who was just trying to sit down at a bar and drink until noon. The jacket was doing the job.

A hover taxi could have shortened the trip, but Jessie needed to get her head in this game. This was a minefield she had no map to navigate, no scanners, no sensors, no tactical analyst on the bridge to give expert advice in real time.

What topics did she need to avoid?

Which topics needed addressing despite being awkward? There wouldn't be room for the two of them if she didn't chase out at least a few of the elephants first.

What state of mind would she find him in?

Jessie hadn't answered any of her questions before Chateau Gateaux appeared in front of her. A full wall of glass panes shaped like large bricks allowed pedestrians to see inside, where a sea of tables showed patrons dining on desserts in the middle of the afternoon. Wooden double doors bound in iron stood open, allowing entry without having to lay siege to the faux castle.

An employee in medieval livery tried to intercept her as she cut the line.

"I'm meeting someone," she informed the host.

On cue, a waving hand caught her eye. The host deferred, and Jessie swerved her way to a table that sat four but only had one person sitting there waiting for her.

Eric Ramsey grinned and got up to crush her in a hug. Well, "crush" might have been an exaggeration. He had a couple centimeters on her, but she could have snapped him in two. "I missed you, Jess."

"Missed you too." Jessie patted him on the back, then they parted and sat on opposite sides of the table.

"This is so great. I know your comms say you're OK, but anyone could be sending those. Seeing you... man. Oh, Jess, it's so nice having you here in the flesh."

She returned what appeared to be a permanent grin on her little brother's face. "Hey, I'm fine. Navy takes good care of me. It's you I worry about."

That melted his grin. "I'm OK. You don't need to... I mean... I'm not in *danger* or anything."

"There's more to being OK than not dying. How you holding up?" That seemed innocuous enough.

"Would you feel better if I lied?"

"I can always tell. Just hit me with it. That's why I'm here."

"Imagine you couldn't be a pilot anymore. What if you weren't allowed on ships at all, and they wanted you to be a farmer?"

Jessie swallowed hard. "That bad, huh? How are classes?"

Her brother produced a datapad and slid it across the table. "I can still barely work this thing, but they want me to program them?"

"Maybe you could get them to try you at something easier."

He scowled. "Easier isn't the point. Once I get all this gizmology lodged in my brain, I won't be dangerous anymore. I won't be *able* to use magic. I'm like Socrates, drinking my own poison."

Jessie fought the urge to squirm in her seat. "How'd it happen?" Might as well rip the slap tape off the wound.

"Got ratted out."

"Ouch."

"You know, you get drunk with your friends, you expect a certain degree of the Vegas Prime Credo to cover you. Except this time, it didn't."

"But what did you *do*?"

"I shouldn't say."

"It's all right," a newcomer interjected. He was an older, dark-skinned fellow with pure white hair. He had a companion, a middle-aged woman with a kind face and hard eyes. "Go ahead and tell her. This is your sister, right?"

Allowing his gaze to fall to the table surface, Eric made a halfhearted flourish toward the pair. "Jessie, allow me to introduce Wizard Jake Snow and Wizard Marissa Slater. Snow... Slater, meet Jessie Ramsey, my older sister."

"Charmed, we're sure," Slater deadpanned.

"Have a seat. Might as well," Eric informed them. The pair had the black-on-black trousers and dress shirt combo accessorized with two hallmarks of wizards: sleeves wide enough to tuck opposing hands into and a garish silver pendant showing a lightning bolt crashing through a letter C. C for 'Convocation,' the preeminent—and only legal—organization of wizards operating in ARGO space.

The wizards dragged themselves into seats, alternating between Convocation lackeys and Ramseys.

Not enjoying the awkward silence that threatened to descend, Jessie broke the ice. "So, how do you guys know each other?"

"They're my parole officers," Eric replied glumly.

"Oh."

"How are your classes going, Eric?" Snow asked in a condescending, paternal tone.

"I'm attending."

"You're not absorbing the material," Slater scolded. "You think we *like* interrupting family reunions?"

"I do get that impression."

Snow grunted. "Well, we don't. Until you get yourself technologified, we're going to be following you around like pocket lint."

"It just doesn't make sense..." Eric whined.

"Hey, lay off him!" Jessie snapped. "He's trying, OK? Maybe he's not cut out for computers."

"We can't let him run around with magic in him. He's a danger. Go on, Eric, tell her why."

Eric glanced up at Jessie without lifting his head. "Time magic."

"Chronomancy!" Snow snapped. "There are few more

forbidden forms of magic. You're only on demagicking parole due to the fact no one got hurt."

"Wait—you, like, time traveled or something?" Jessie wasn't sure what went on at universities that offered classes in magic, but that wasn't on the syllabus she imagined.

"I didn't!" Eric protested. "I was just doodling."

Slater shook her head. "It was more than doodling. I hear it was plausible."

"You hear?" Jessie echoed. "You haven't even seen it?"

"Above our pay grade," Snow explained. "Senior librarians only."

"And four undergrads," Slater added. "All of whom are under surveillance for signs that they might recall those glyphs of yours."

"What the hell, Eric?"

"It was cocktail napkins. It's crazy. There are three honest-to-Merlin cocktail napkins from Cosmic Drake's Pub locked up in the Vault of the Plundered Tomes."

"They belong there, and you should be thankful you were just expelled. They got to you in time. Whoever informed the dean did you a huge favor." Snow pushed back his chair and stood. "But we're not here to share an overpriced cake. This fulfills your check-in for the week. I, uh, suppose you'll be looking for *us* to pick up the tab?"

Eric shook his head. "This is a family affair."

Jessie leaned forward and spoke through her teeth. "I hope you're not expecting *me* to foot this if these clowns are offering."

But Eric was already waving goodbye, and the wizards disappeared into the crowd of patrons.

For the first time, Jessie had a good look at the dishes the other tables were receiving. The cakes were sculptures, each a legitimate piece of artwork, all edible and delicious based on the reactions on all sides of them. At the table beside them, a conspicuously wealthy family of four cut up a chocolate cityscape on a ganache oceanside. To the other side, a couple on a date enjoyed a red velvet heart that stood upright, at least 25 centimeters tall. A waitress breezed past bearing a platter upon which two confectionary lovers entwined.

"Quit worrying."

"Don't tell me *you're* paying."

Eric shook his head, his mischievous grin returning. "You really *don't* keep in touch with the family, do you?"

"Dad win the Solar Lottery or something?"

"No, this is Aunt Michelle's new restaurant." He pointed. Jessie followed his finger and caught sight of Aunt Michelle when the swinging doors to the kitchen swung open. "She invited us over for drinks after closing."

"You drink now?"

"Soda for me. But she was excited to hear you were coming."

"Wow. Just... good for her! About time she caught a big break like this." Aunt Michelle had started five or six restaurants by now, none of which had caught fire—well, except one that had *literally*. But Chateau Gateaux seemed like it was thriving.

Jessie glanced back, checking to see whether either of Eric's parole officers had stuck around. "Tell me, was that whole spiel true? Or did you, like, fuck the dean's wife or something?"

"Ha. Ha."

"OK, fine. Sorry. But seriously, that sounds less unlikely than getting expelled for—what did he call it?—chronomancy?"

A waitress showed up, dropped off a couple sodas, and departed. Jessie found that hers was cherry cola, and she grinned at Eric's thoughtfulness—unless it had been Aunt Michelle who'd remembered.

"It was all theoretical. Mostly."

"Mostly?"

"A minute. It was by myself. No witnesses. I was just trying to explain how it worked, and I was trying to work out how to go backward—which is way harder."

"And you got burned by one of your friends."

"Maybe the bartender," Eric replied lamely. "I thought Doris was blasty, but maybe I wasn't the *best* tipper. I wasn't rich like most of the other students, so—"

"Eric, what are you planning to do now?" Jessie couldn't help it. There were so many other topics, but a sisterly concern for her brother's well-being just wouldn't let her ignore the one she found most pressing. She couldn't be like Mom and Dad and just let him roll along with whichever way the wind blew. He was a person, not a tumbleweed.

"I was planning on a nice dinner with no nutritious value, then hanging out with Aunt Michelle and Uncle Damon, then heading back to my apartment to sleep on the couch while you take the bed."

"Big picture. You know what I mean. Where do you see yourself five years from now?"

"Why so long?"

"Because. Without a plan for the future, you'll just get stuck living meal to meal, class to class, doing whatever someone else tells you?"

"What do you think I should do?"

"That's a cop-out. You need to *want* something."

"I want to be a wizard." It was Eric's turn to glance around, paranoid. "I figure if I can pass some classes, get Snow and Slater off my back, maybe I can re-wrinkle the parts of my brain they want me to smooth out."

Jessie tried not to judge. She could only imagine the allure of not playing by the laws of physics, of treating gravity and momentum like starting points of a negotiation. But there wasn't a place in society for wizards who didn't play by the Convocation's rules. The only options were playing by Sir Isaac Newton's rules, the Convocation's, or... "I don't know if you'd make it living as an outlaw. No offense."

"None taken. That's really kind of you to say."

Jessie squinted. It hadn't been a compliment. "I just mean, you don't really have that killer instinct, that cut-and-run or stay-and-fight trigger that Dad has. Or even Uncle Enzio."

"I know you don't think much of me. But I'm not hopeless."

"I just think you sort of take life in stride. If Uncle Enzio hadn't written that letter of recommendation, do you think you'd have gone to college at all?"

Eric shrugged and didn't look up. That was when she noticed that he was scribbling on the little napkin that came with their drinks. "I've always wanted you to be proud of me."

"Can you just play along? Think about it: what would you do to be where you want to be five years from now?"

"What's that got to do with anything?" He continued his doodling. He'd always been one to get lost in his own little world. It was progress that he could keep up his half of a conversation.

"Everything. Look, five years ago, I was a recruit. No college. Failed the Annapolis entry exams. But I graded out on the flight test, sharpshooting, survival, mechanics, tactics. I knew I wanted to work special ops—"

Eric glanced up suddenly. His eyes lit. "You're a commando?"

Well, technically, her role wasn't top secret, even if every little thing she did might have been. Jessie nodded. "That's why I don't get a lot of leave. Always a mission. Or a certification. Or a training course."

"Mom must be so proud!"

"I haven't told them. I don't want Mom to worry."

"Come on. They'd love to know."

"Point is, I had a five-year plan, and it only ended up taking me three. And if yours is to weasel out of Convocation parole... well, there's a start."

"I have more of a one-second plan at the moment."

"Huh?"

Eric turned his napkin 180 degrees and slid it across to her. "Voila."

"What's this? No. Please don't tell me it's—"

"Yup."

"This isn't funny."

"One second. One measly second. People will do a double-take, but no one's going to *really* notice."

Jessie shook her head emphatically. "Someone will see. Or have a camera out."

"No one sees magic on a camera. It's the holovid paradox. Any time you see magic in a holo, you know it's fake. If they showed a blur, you'd stop thinking the holovid was real, breaking your immersion."

"Look, if you don't want to work on a five-year plan, we'll drop it. Let's just order some cake."

"Take my hand."

"Why?"

"To prove to you I'm not just a screwup. You're trying to fix the only thing that's not broken about me. Unless a big, tough Earth Navy commando is *scared*..." He singsonged it like they were still kids.

Jessie smirked at the transparent attempt at manipulation. Eric wasn't like Dad. He was the kind of kid who'd get pulled over for a traffic violation and talk his way into additional fines —if he had a pilot's license.

Fine. What was one second going to hurt? More than likely,

his spell would do nothing. After all, from the parole officers' reaction, this was not-for-shitters magic, and Eric had been taking programming classes lately, even if he was failing them.

She promised herself to be nice when he failed.

Jessie took the offered hand.

Eric placed his other hand over the napkin, closed his eyes. His lips moved as he muttered nonsense.

Jessie felt a tingle. Just as she was about to pull her hand away in panic, purple flames crawled out from under Eric's hand as the napkin burned away.

Then there was a sensation of falling.

⸺

"Oops."

The word escaped Eric's lips involuntarily. It was one among his many failings as a young wizard. A good wizard kept his words caged like inmates, only paroling them when prudent. He was, as he had just demonstrated yet again, the other sort.

"Ha. Ha," Jessie deadpanned from across the table. She looked all around them, scanning the now-vacant restaurant. Tables and chairs were scattered about the dining area with no discernible pattern, some toppled or broken. The lights were dead; if not for gaps in the slap tape plastering the windows, the Ramsey siblings would have been in pitch darkness.

"Sorry. I think I undersold this." Eric cleared his throat. "Oh, shit."

"How'd you do it? Is this all an illusion?" Jessie reached out to her side, tentatively, as if expecting at any moment to collide with an unseen restaurant patron. "Did you mess with my head? You *better* not have messed with my head. That's a felony, considering my clearance level."

Eric let his eyes do the searching of their surroundings, barely daring to budge. "This isn't a joke."

His sister smirked. "It better be. If you really destroyed Aunt Michelle's restaurant—"

"I didn't. At least, not directly."

The smile vanished. "Eric, you're starting to freak me out here. Come clean. This is just magic, right?"

"Magic? Yes. Just? No. Right? Definitely not."

"Stop that!" Jessie snapped.

"Stop what?"

"The word thing. This is *not* the time for the word thing."

"I wasn't doing the word thing. You asked a nuanced question and I answered thoroughly."

Jessie stood and bracketed her face with her hands. "Here's a nice, simple, straightforward question: what the *fuck* did you do?"

Multiple potential ways to answer her flashed through Eric's mind in succession, each accompanied by preliminary hand gestures and an opening of the mouth but no actual sounds. Finally, he settled on, "I'm not quite sure."

The tension in his sister's jaw reminded Eric of the old days growing up together. She was always the one who took charge, got stressed out, somehow pulled everything together.

For the time being, he let her go with her instinct. She patrolled the dining area with a cursory sort of thoroughness, going behind the counter in case anyone might be hiding there, poking a head into the kitchen.

Eric followed at a distance that suggested he didn't want to get in her way but supported her efforts.

"What the fuck?" she muttered.

Then Jessie headed for the main doors. They didn't open at her approach. Since the rest of the science in the building didn't appear to be functioning, that wasn't so surprising. Her attempt to get her fingers into the seam between doors ended in nothing but frustrated grunting and half-voiced swearing.

"Do you mind?" She stepped aside and swept a hand at the doors.

Eric flashed a close-lipped smile. With a flick of the fingers on both hands, the restaurant doors burst open.

Streetlights flooded in. Hovers raced past. It was the dead of night, and New Shanghai was hopping.

Jessie backpedaled away from the door. When Eric lingered, she dragged him back with her.

"WHAT DID YOU DO?"

"I opened the doors. Wasn't that what you—?"

"Before. The big 'oops.' What the fuck is going on here?"

Eric swallowed. "What day is it?"

Jessie ducked out of sight and grabbed Eric to drag him with her. They leaned back against the wall. Eric found a bench seat meant for patrons awaiting a table and slumped onto it.

His sister joined him. "It's February 10th, 2586. I know because I had to punch it in on my leave request. Today, being the first day of my first vacation in God-knows-how-long, it stuck."

"Can you... double-check that?"

Jessie fixed him with a laser-beam scowl but dug out her datapad nonetheless. She looked at the blank screen. Then poked and prodded the device. "It's dead. You fuzzled it."

"Sorry."

"Why do you think I might be wrong about the date?" Her words carried a mom-like threat of repercussions for an errant answer.

"I just want to check before I venture any guesses."

"You have a theory. I can tell. You're a paper book."

"Open book," Eric corrected.

"Books don't open unless they're paper. Now, spit it out."

"I was aiming for a one-second little blip."

"Yeah. Clearly, something went wrong. We were out for hours."

"I didn't lose consciousness," Eric assured her. "I don't think you did, either."

"There's no way to be certain. By the look of it, you zapped us for maybe... I dunno, five, six hours?" She frowned as if she'd started listening to her own words. "But if we were unconscious in the middle of a restaurant, they'd have rushed us to a hospital, not evacuated and left us. Unless something *else* happened, too. Did you, I don't know, summon a demon to watchdog for us?"

"I don't know any demons."

"Right. Demons aren't real. Shit. What the hell happened in those six hours?"

Eric barred his lips with a finger. The gesture ought to have appeared thoughtful, but it was more a reminder to give this matter its full pondering before voicing his theory.

"What was the last thing you said to me before the spell?" Apparently, Eric was fully capable of speaking past a finger.

"Why?" she replied after a brief pause for contemplation.

"Just humor me."

"No, that's what I said: 'Why?'"

"Yeah. Right. Sorry. Before that?"

Jessie stewed a moment. "I said if you don't want to talk about it, let's just order some cake."

"Talk about what?"

"Coming up with a five-year plan. Really, is this going somewhere?"

Eric tapped the fingertips of each hand against those of the other. "That's the thing. I think maybe that five-year plan might have been on *my* mind."

"Eriiiiiiic..."

"It's a theory!" He scooted away, taking advantage of the bench's length, meant for allowing whole families to loiter for want of a reservation.

"There's something you're not telling me."

Eric pointed to the open door. "Down the street. Ad board. The Marcie Mason holo."

Without asking for clarification, Jessie got up and edged over to the doorway. Gingerly, Eric followed.

At first, when she peeked around the corner, Jessie said nothing. Eric watched her face. He spotted the instant it sank in, the instant she spotted the release date for Marcie Mason's latest holovid. Eric peeked around beside his sister and double-checked for himself.

CLEO VS. ATTILA, starring MARCIE MASON, OPENING TOMORROW: FEB 11, 2591.

━━━

"OK. Things could be worse."

Eric spoke these words with two fistfuls of his shirt in his sister's firm possession. His back was jammed against the restaurant wall, and he was up on tiptoe to spare her the strain of supporting his entire weight.

"Explain to me how this could be worse."

Eric cleared his throat, always ready for a challenge. "Well, Marcie Mason's career seems to have bounced back from *Month With No Name.*" He gestured toward the ad board, barely able to reach the open door with his wrist.

Jessie gritted her teeth. "This. Is. SERIOUS! If you magicked us five years into the future—"

"For argument's sake, let's not call that one an 'if.'"

"Then we are in a *galaxy* of shit!"

"Well, I might be. You should be fine. After all, you're not on probation and forbidden from having magic used *on* you. I, for one, am in line to be fitted for a bonfire."

Jessie cocked her head. "You don't get it, do you? I'm on leave. Or I was. And why was it hard for me to find time for leave? Because I'm in a high-profile unit."

"Which you can't even name."

"Within Earth Navy, dorkface. And thanks to you, I'm AWOL."

Eric scowled at this. "If you don't quit shoving, it's me who's going to be part of a wall."

With a final push that both admitted he was right and refused to admit it aloud, Jessie released her brother. "Absent without leave. Deserted. Right up there with treason and piracy, it's the only way to get yourself spaced by a navy captain."

"You didn't desert. I can explain everything."

"Sure. Right. Time magic. The only ones who'd believe that would skin you alive for doing it."

Eric's scowl only deepened. "Well, that's no good. I'm just going to have to find a way to undo this mess." He pushed up his sleeves.

Reacting quicker than he'd have expected, Jessie grabbed those sleeves and yanked them back down. "No. I don't know what the fuck you did to get us here—"

"Overexuberant chronomancy."

"We're finding an expert to fix it."

Eric blinked. She was looking him right in the eye, a level of trust a sister shouldn't have in a wizard brother. He was the one who shied away. "It's possible that..." He hesitated. Putting words to his notion might ruin everything, might solidify a horrifying truth into crystalline reality.

"Possible what? That this was a giant illusion that fooled us both? That we'll snap back to our own time if we hang in there? That the Convocation's got a temporal rescue squad in their back pocket? What?"

"... that I *am* the expert."

━━━

They couldn't stay at the restaurant. Any potential to discover clues within the abandoned building balanced poorly against the chance that authorities would show up to investigate. While Jessie was vaguely worried that some nosy wizard would have noticed whatever-the-fuck Eric had done, the fact that they'd opened the doors of a vacant building and potentially been spotted by regular old everyday busybodies meant that they were already on someone's scanners.

Mars, which moments ago had felt so glittering and civilized, now pressed around her with a sinister presence. The hairs at the back of Jessie's neck prickled. She tucked her hands in the pockets of her jacket and kept her head down. Eyes seemed to follow them wherever she glanced.

"Wow, half a decade really overhauled this place," Eric commented, gawking like a tourist in a city that had been his home for months.

"Don't draw attention to yourself," she warned.

"Looking like you don't want people to look at you is making them look at you."

"I'm minding my own business. Mind yours."

Ignoring her utterly, Eric waved to a group of youths who stared openly in their direction. "Hi, guys. Nice night in good old New Shanghai. Am I right?"

"Would you quit it?"

He lowered his voice. "It's a friendly city. Safe. Lots of security. In fact, way more than yesterday."

Jessie's mouth had gone dry. She didn't know this place like Eric, but she'd suspected the same thing. This wasn't a normal look for a core world, let alone Mars. Businesses had uniformed nobodies stationed at their doors as bouncers with stun blasters. She'd noticed civilians with blasters strapped at their sides. Though she hadn't spotted one yet herself, the way people kept sneaking glances toward the sky suggested aerial surveillance drones.

A security guard in front of one of the local pastry shops lifted a middle finger. If there was any question of where his gesture was aimed, he made it clear when he slowly tracked Jessie and Eric's progress down the sidewalk.

"Yeah, well, we're on the street with no place we belong. New Shanghai looks like it's had an underhaul. I don't know what's going on, but I don't like being out on the streets unarmed."

"We're not unarmed."

"I didn't even bring a sidearm on this trip. I'm not a magic suitcase full of guns, like in the holos." Of course, if she had access to her hotel room from five years ago, there was a blaster there. She just hadn't planned to need her luggage to meet Eric for dessert.

"I'm a you-know-what, after all."

"Idiot?" Jessie snarked out of reflex. She wouldn't have said it to anyone but a fresh recruit while in uniform, but Eric was her kid brother. He occupied a unique niche in her life.

Eric cleared his throat. "Rhymes with a bad snowstorm?"

Jessie's mind wandered two directions at once. She couldn't concentrate on her brother's nonsense—not fully, at any rate—while they were adrift in an alternate timeline. New Shanghai felt hostile, and she trusted her instincts enough to heed that sensation of animosity that pressed from all sides. "Mad glow dorm?"

"Excellent penmanship. Monastic fashion sensibilities."

Two guys in a parked hover watched, following them with their eyes, heads slowly turning in unison.

"Try to keep focused. We could be in real danger here."

On an upper floor of a building across the street, a silhouetted figure ducked out of sight. Then the window went dark.

"Better-than-average bowler."

Jessie pulled up short. "You can't be serious."

"I can protect us. Relax. Maybe the time stream will snap us right back to where we belong. At least make sure you get home with a story to tell."

"Eric. I love you. But you flunked out of college."

A mother and her two young children were approaching them down the sidewalk. When she spotted them in return, she shepherded her kids to the nearest crossing and switched sides of the road.

"Expulsion isn't a failing grade," Eric countered.

Jessie kept the mother in the corner of her view until doing so would have required her to turn her head. What the hell was up with these people?

"It's not a ringing endorsement either."

A hover swooped down from the overhead traffic, pulling up to the curb alongside them. It was a Kroger LeTour that had to have been fifteen—make that twenty—years old and looked every day of it by the wear and tear. Reverb units on the ion exhaust set Jessie's back teeth on edge as it rumbled to an idle.

Windows slid open on the side. College-age kids leaned out, one shirtless, one wearing a New Shanghai Knights jersey, another in a sweat-stained tank top.

"Mars first! Mars forever!"

"WooooOOOOooooOOO!"

"Run, little kitties! Mars belongs to the dogs!"

The hover jetted back into the sky before Jessie could shout after them, asking what the hell drugs they were on.

"Kitties?" She asked Eric. He was a new resident, but he had to have been more up on Martian slang than her.

"New one to me. But I think it was you they were yelling at."

"Guys that age, they'd have made it sexual if they were hollering my way."

"I'm that age."

"You're an odd duck. Strike that; you're an odd platypus."

Jessie led them into a public park. If nothing else, it was semi-restricted airspace, limiting the options for yahoos to buzz them without getting doinked by New Shanghai traffic cops.

She turned the words over in her head. It was the "Mars first" bit that stood out. Slipping out her datapad, she checked it again. The device had yet to recover from its time-traveling adventure.

"No luck?" Eric asked, peering nosily over her shoulder.

"Think you might have dusted it."

"Sorry."

"Well, something's going on here on Mars. Maybe just New Shanghai. Either way, I need the omni to figure out what's up, and I don't have data access."

Eric pointed to a knot of people huddled under a gazebo. They looked rough, but it was hard to tell. Maybe fashion had drifted that direction in five years.

As they passed a small building that housed public washrooms, Jessie spotted a guy heading inside.

Something in her tactical brain catalogued a trio of traits that marked this poor random dude as a target.

First, he was packing. Martians had overcome their longstanding shyness about open carry of blasters on city streets, and that had extended to their parks as well. She couldn't ID the model, but the bulge at the back of his belt was unmistakable beneath his jacket.

Second, the guy was throwing clear civilian vibes. Casual, lackadaisical, entitled, presuming a level of safety just for being a taxpayer.

Third, and this could not be discounted in her calculus, he was wearing a leather jacket that looked about her size.

"Hang here a minute," Jessie instructed her brother.

The not-quite-wizard blinked free of whatever reverie had kept him quiet these past few minutes. He registered the washroom shack, and understanding dawned. "Now that you mention it, I could—"

"No. Just wait here."

"But it's a pee-for-all. We could both just—"

"Wait. Here. I'll be back fast."

Eric gave her a concerned scowl, but she'd endured worse from better emotional manipulators. Jessie made a beeline for the washrooms before she lost her window of opportunity.

Moments later, she emerged.

"What happened to your jacket?" Eric asked.

"I traded it."

"And where'd you get that datapad?" he followed up, nodding at the new device in her hands.

She didn't look up as it connected to an omni news service she trusted. "Part of the same trade."

"You're not fooling anyone," Eric pressed. He fell in step as she started off, not wanting to be anywhere nearby when aftermaths and consequences came looking. "Is he okay?"

The jacket's former owner was head first in a toilet sniffing antibacterial fumes in his sleep. Her former datapad was in the washroom waste reclaim with a few plasma holes through the data core. The jacket with the Earth Navy patches on it had been stuffed down after it. Only one of the three was liable to complain about their treatment.

"He's fine. Shit. But I think we might not be."

"Why's that?"

"Glad I ditched the jacket," Jessie replied as she angled the datapad for Eric to see. He might not have been much for *using* a datapad, but reading text on a screen meshed well with a wizard's specialties.

Via the Orion News Network, the headline read: Earth and Mars Clashes Expand in Borderlands as Civil War Enters Fourth Year.

"Apparently, we're the enemy."

"Who's we?" Eric demanded haughtily. "I'm a resident."

"Doubt that'll count for much if someone with a pointy hat comes looking."

The park had taken on a sinister aspect now that Jessie understood the scope of their dilemma. What the hell had happened in the five missing years? Clearly, some of the shit that bubbled under the surface of ARGO life had erupted with sufficient force to sunder not only the interspecies alliance but Solar unity as well.

Right now, none of that mattered.

"We need to get off the streets."

"This is a public park. We're on a paved walkway within sight of honest-to-Artemis ducks." Eric pointed, and lo and behold, there indeed was a gaggle of ducks floating on an artificial pond. The water couldn't have been more than a couple hectares, and the odds of those ducks surviving in the wild were slim. But Eric's point stood; they weren't exactly standing in traffic.

"Consider it a term of art. We're in public. We're being seen without seeing by who."

"Whom."

"We need a safe house. We need intel on the situation. Ninety percent chance we need passage off Mars."

"To where?"

Jessie took a turn and guided them deeper into the interior of the park. It wasn't getting them off the streets, but the towering, manicured trees offered a modicum of concealment from distant surveillance.

"Doesn't matter. Secondary problem. Better question, do you have any money?"

Eric shrugged. "Enough to feed those ducks if Mr. Stennek is still around here selling croutons." He peered around with a sweeping glance.

"Knock it off with the ducks."

"You brought them up. That's why we came this way. You made me want to see ducks."

"I didn't even know there were waterfowl in this park when I..." She trailed off. "I'm leading the way, right?"

Eric nodded, maybe just a little too quickly. "Definitely."

This wasn't the time to argue. Either Eric was a fuckup who'd gotten booted out of school or a mastermind altering Jessie's thoughts without her noticing. Accidentally punting them five years into the future strongly hinted at a lack of control.

"First things first, we need to get the lay of the land—politically," she amended quickly. "Last thing I need is a geography lesson."

"Geography's bunk anyway. Geonomy's the good stuff."

"Where can we find a safe place to eat, sleep, and shower?" she blurted before her aether-headed brother hauled them into yet another pointless debate of minutiae.

"What about Auntie Michelle's place?"

"It was dead. Remember?"

"You can't *live* in a restaurant. She and Damon have a nice little apartment."

OK. Finally. A solid plan. Whatever shit might be going down, Aunt Michelle was a Ramsey by blood, and Ramseys stuck together. Well, other than that thing between Dad and Grampa Chuck.

"Fine. Where's their apartment?"

Eric pointed over his shoulder. "Back the way we came. Actually, it was only a couple blocks from the restaurant."

⊏⊐

Eric led the way with a certainty that he hoped convinced Jessie (and anyone who might be spying on them) that he was a bona fide resident of New Shanghai. And while it was the middle of the night, science glows lit the way with usual technological efficiency.

"Huh. Right over there, where you see that Mexican pizza place, used to be this great little Italian place that made the best breadsticks. I wonder if the war had anything to do with them closing or if they just gave away too many breadsticks to all-you-can-eat wizards. Or... maybe it was a *lack* of hungry wizards that—"

"Watch where we're going," Jessie snapped, grabbing him by the sleeve.

Eric returned his attention forward and saw a gaggle of men who were either economically disadvantaged or dressed the part out of some new fashion trend. They blocked the sidewalk, laughing amongst themselves and sharing a scarce supply of liquor that they passed back and forth.

"What? They're happy. I don't see a problem." He kept

going. Realizing that Jessie was a worrier, he lowered his voice and tried to keep his lips from moving. "Just don't spook them."

"We should find another route."

"But this is the shortest—" A jerk on the sleeve his sister still held diverted him forcibly from his course.

"We're going around."

Eric raised a wave. "Sorry, guys. Just showing my sister around."

"What the fuck?" Jessie demanded. "Are you looking to get us killed?"

Eric didn't back down. "You were being rude. Eduardo and Van are good guys."

"You *know* those guys?"

"Not all of them. Van cooks at a ramen bar I go to on Tuesdays. Eduardo is a life counselor at the college."

"A life counselor..."

Eric rolled his eyes. "It's not my business what he does in his off hours. The New Shanghai Basic Skills Empowerment Academy isn't exactly full of students who've made great life choices."

Jessie released his sleeve and stopped trying to steer him like a hover-cart.

"You could have said something sooner," Jessie grumbled. She pretended it was beneath her breath, but Eric knew he was meant to hear. "Still, being ID'ed on the street is bad news."

"No better or worse than running into an old friend in the park while you were trading in the washroom."

Jessie's eyes shot wide. Then she saw Eric's smirk.

She backhanded him in the chest. "Don't do that!"

"You're really tense. We're on an adventure. Look. It's not what either of us expected to be doing today—or even expected today to be happening so soon—and I'm sorry about that. But let's make the best of it. Auntie Michelle can catch us up on the news. I'll check in with my parole wizards; you'll write a nice comm to Earth Navy about why you disappeared. Everything will work itself out."

They crossed a pedestrian bridge over Jinsan Avenue, sandwiched between ground and aerial traffic. Jessie couldn't wait to be indoors and free from public observation.

"Literally none of that is true."

"You *are* tense."

"I am a measured and situationally appropriate degree of alert."

Eric pointed. "That's her place, up ahead."

The vantage from the bridge afforded a view of a balconied apartment tower overlooking a civic reservoir.

"Not bad."

"It's pretty great. Auntie Michelle's got a professional kitchen and a special case that cools bottles of wine to *just* the right temperature. And the couch folds out into a pretty comfortable bed."

"You stayed with her?"

"Them. Uncle Damon lives there, too. And it was only for a few weeks before I got settled and my student housing stipend started coming in."

They descended to street level on the far side of the bridge, destination in sight just a couple blocks away.

"Why didn't you just hit up Mom and Dad?"

How could he even start? From the I-told-you-sos from Mom and the oblique job offers from Dad to rope him into a life of crime, the subtle condescension of Roddy, or the aspirational voyeurism of Yomin inquiring about his nonexistent love life, there were a million reasons Jessie wouldn't understand.

Luckily, growing up a Ramsey meant having a convenient excuse at hand, especially one that wasn't a lie while, at the same time, not exactly being the truth, either. "I'm not supposed to be associating with wizards," he replied after a thoughtful pause.

Jessie snorted. "Uncle Enzio barely qualifies. I bet you they'd have given you special dispensation if—"

Eric stopped short. "They wouldn't have. Uncle Enzio may just be a cranky old beer-summoner to you, but he was my mentor. My pre-collegiate teacher of Convocation record. I am a blood mark on his career. If he even wants to *talk* to me anymore, I'd be hurting his reputation just by being seen with him."

Jessie had turned away halfway through his rant.

"Sorry. I've never been able to wrap my head around that whole student/mentor thing. Didn't mean to pick at a fresh scab."

Eric huffed and started back off toward Auntie Michelle's house.

"It's not fresh. It's been over five years."

━━

Eric knocked at the door.

Jessie shouldered her way in front of him to press the chime.

Her brother huffed a passive-aggressive little sigh. "The knock told her it was me."

Jessie kept her voice down. "And make her suspicious as fuck when her dead nephew shows up."

"That's a conversation we're going to get no matter what. Five years is longer than Dad's fake-your-death buffer."

Jessie cast him an immediate scowl. "How'd you know about that? It was a secret between him and me."

"Dad has that 'secret' with everyone. I'm almost surprised he included you."

Jessie laughed. "Really? Me? I'm more surprised that—"

The door slid open.

"Oh. Hello," Eric greeted the person who answered—a person who was neither Aunt Michelle nor Uncle Damon.

The older woman at the door glowered at them, stern, stout, and sturdy, wearing rumpled pajamas and an overnight hairdo helmet. "Who're you with?"

"Um, I'm looking for Michelle Carlito. About yea tall, long curly hair, usually smells of pastry flour." Eric still held his hand out from his estimate of Aunt Michelle's height.

"Never heard of her."

"Owner of the Chateau Gateaux," Eric persisted. The woman at the door didn't show a flinch of understanding. If this had been an Earth Navy interrogation, Jessie would have admired her resolve in withholding information. "Owned a Pekingese with a pink mohawk."

A slight frown darkened the pajama-clad woman's features. "Go sober up. Take those Earth accents and scram. You got the wrong place."

"I'm perfectly—erp."

Jessie yanked her brother clear of the door, flashing a perfunctory smile. "Sorry to bother you, ma'am. We must have gotten the wrong address."

It felt weird manhandling her brother, now that Eric was about her size. If any of his matching bulk had been muscle, he might have put up a struggle.

"It's not the wrong address," Eric insisted once the door closed and they were safe from eavesdropping. "She hasn't even changed the doormat. There's Pekingese fur trampled into the pile."

"Right place, wrong time. Clearly, Auntie Michelle's

business troubles spilled over into personal finances. They probably had to move somewhere cheaper."

Eric blinked. "Is it expensive here?"

"Yah. How can you not tell?"

"The Convocation pays my rent and tuition so I don't try to earn money doing magic." He jangled a chain that disappeared beneath his shirt. "I only ever pay for food."

"Well, we still have the problem of finding shelter without accessing digital funds."

They emerged back onto the city streets, lost in time, if not location. Eric's intel on New Shanghai was like old milk, usable but maybe too dangerous to trust. What they needed was *someone*, whether it was Auntie Michelle or not, who could give them the break they needed to catch their breath.

"What about Mom and Dad?" Eric suggested. His constipated expression conveyed his reluctance to admit the shitstorm they'd gotten into.

Not that Jessie relished the verbal beatdown that would follow. On the one hand, fair was fair. Mom, Dad, and Ozzy deserved to know the two of them were alive. Alive and *well* would have been a lie, though, and without even knowing what sector they might be in, any forthcoming help would be marginal at best.

Ozzy. Wow. Their little brother wouldn't be so much littler anymore. He'd be what... nineteen? For the first time in his life, they might be able to relate on equal terms—not that Jessie suspected him of turning into a time-traveling commando behind enemy lines during the five-year gap.

Then again, they might have a current address for Auntie Michelle.

A moment later, it dawned on her.

"We *do* know someone else on Mars. Someone who

probably *hasn't* crashed into a financial asteroid and had to hit the escape pods."

"Oh. Right. Duh."

Jessie felt a spring in her step with a renewed sense of purpose. "If Aunt Esper can't help us out, no one can."

They strode off into the Martian night.

━━━

Jessie loitered across the street from the Ya Ya Gou nightclub, whose funny name always gave Eric a chuckle. If he paused to consider, he was loitering too. A legalistic view might reduce the charge to accessory to loitering, since he was only here keeping an eye on his sister, but realistically, few law enforcement sorts seemed likely to split that hair with him.

Every time the door to the club opened or closed, corny old music spilled forth, along with the amateur vocal stylings of karaoke singers. Of course, this being late in the clubbing evening, patrons exited that same door, in groups or—most frequently—in pairs.

Though he'd never been inside, this wasn't the first time Eric had lingered within view of the entrance, watching the colorful parade. Because, unlike many similar establishments, Ya Ya Gou was a costume ball every night. The dress code was animal mascot, but beyond that guideline, creativity reigned.

A blue-furred wolf exited arm in arm with a clearly inebriated unicorn. A gorilla ambled out, affecting a bow-legged gait. A pink-and-black-striped tiger bowed to a human-looking valet as he accepted help with the door to his hover.

"Wipe that dumb grin off your face," Jessie ordered.

Was he smiling? A quick check confirmed that, yes, he indeed was. "Sorry. It's just... Look at them all. The wonder of it..."

"You're literally a wizard. That's fabric and plastic."

"... the smiles..."

"The masks are smiling. Or helmets. Or whatever-the-fuck you call them."

"... you can tell they're happy by the body language."

"That's inebriation. Those human-sized pets are wasted."

Eric shook his head. She didn't understand. "I come down here when I need to see humanity overcoming its inherent sadness."

Jessie pointed to a person in a chimp suit, dangling his arms and scratching his pits. "And most of those costumes are more than a little xenoist."

With a little sigh, Eric gave ground. "Fine. Some of them. A little." He swept a hand before Jessie pulled it back down. "You can't be wildly inclusionary without letting in some bad eggs."

"Well, tonight, we're going to be a couple of those bad eggs."

"Aww."

"What? Are they friends of yours?"

"I don't know; they're all in disguise."

Jessie backed around the corner of the chess cafe whose streetlamp shadows they'd been lingering within. Eric followed into the little alleyway used by employees and waste-reclaim drones.

All the best illicit plans took place aboard disreputable little starships. Lived experience confirmed that. But the Hollyworld vision of clandestine plotting in the gaps between city buildings held up as a reasonable second place. Besides, they were short precisely one ship to make the other method work.

"What's your plan?" Eric asked with resignation.

"Step one is drop the attitude."

"I can see where this is going. You're about to involve innocent people."

"No one's going to get hurt."

"Unless they object to getting their hover stolen. Or they're angry drunks. Or one's an off-duty peace officer. Or something—Merlin forbid—doesn't go exactly according to plan."

Jessie pressed him against the wall with her forearm, staring him down from a nose-length away. Eric glanced aside for her own protection. "Look. We're in a bind here. If we don't get sheltered soon—or, better yet, out of Sol entirely—we're in for a galaxy of shit."

"We seem fine so far. Maybe they didn't notice." That seemed like a stretch. Unless all Martian wizards had packed up and left, plenty of people would have noticed that kind of arcane disruption.

"That's because we're getting zero intel," Jessie countered, still pinning him in place like that was the only way she'd have his full attention. "But we're leaking fuel. It started when we dropped into this timeline, and we've been dripping the whole way from there to here. Eyes on Aunt Michelle's bakery when we opened the door. Your noodle-slinging friend. The woman who lives in Michelle and Damon's old place. Someone's going to investigate, find the start of our trail, and light it on fire. Quicker than you can imagine, that trail's going to burn right up until it engulfs us."

"I have a pretty good imagination."

Jessie leaned back, releasing Eric. "You'd better, because we need costumes."

Unbidden, a smile came to his face. "Really? I never pictured you as the type to—"

"For the mission," she assured him. "The plan is simple. We poke in for a bit; come back out. Loiter a little. Then we latch onto someone coming out for the valet."

"Who?"

"I'll do the picking. I know what to look for. I just need you to make us look like *them*." She pointed back at the agglomeration of animal-costumed revelers.

"I thought about buying a costume at one point, but money's a little tight, and you'd be surprised how much one of those—"

"Magic. Just use illusions."

"I can't. They have rules against—oh. Wait. I guess if we're not obeying *laws*, why would we bother with rules? I guess I could. Illusions aren't my specialty."

"Just like when we were kids. Simple stuff, right?"

Eric watched the comings and goings at the club, mind already wandering to the images he might conjure. "You know... someday, I'd like to meet the version of me that lives in your head." Then, the answer clicked. More precisely, it *pinged*, like the sound of a fork tapping the side of a drinking glass. "OK. I think I've got it. Any last-minute requests?"

With the shuddering breath a person not looking forward to being magicked, Jessie steeled herself. "I honestly don't give a shit. Just something that's not too big to fit into a civilian hover. Oh, and I definitely need to be able to steer."

Eric shut his eyes for the duration of a finger snap, picturing in full detail what he wanted. When he opened his eyes, Jessie was no longer the sister he'd grown up with.

"Whoa."

"You like?"

Jessie twisted and flexed, getting as good a look at her new appearance as she could without the aid of a mirror. "What am I wearing?"

"For you, I went with a teal-furred fox in a vintage school uniform. I call the look 'kitsune kawaii.'"

Jessie tilted her vulpine face to look down the bridge of her elongated nose at him. "For how quick that was, you sound like you put a lot of thought into this." Then, she took a good look at him. "And what's with you?"

"I'm a meerkat," Eric proclaimed. He shuffled in a circle to let her get a good look at him. "And, with the kaffiyeh and robe, I'm an emir meerkat."

Jessie rolled her oversized eyes at him. "Fine. Let's go. We look ridiculous."

"We fit in."

"Whatever. I gotta say, this costume's got better field of vision than I expected."

Eric fought back a smirk. "What can I say? Magic's pretty good stuff."

He followed his sister across the street. They met no resistance at the door.

Inside, fur-clad partygoers frolicked and sang along to creaky old Earth tunes. Some danced on the central floor. Others lounged on couches or crowded into booths. Usually, in a crowd, people instinctively avoided bodily contact. Here, as soon as they were inside, Jessie and Eric were rubbed against and petted on all sides.

They didn't linger. Eric sang along with two karaoke favorites. Jessie swiped a shot glass and downed its contents with its owner none the wiser. Then, with a nudge and an insistent jerk of her furry head, Jessie directed them back out.

"Got a scan?" a young valet asked when they didn't depart the area out front.

"Waiting for some friends," Jessie answered back.

Groups left the club as the entertainment died down for the night. Time and again, Eric tried to prod his sister to action. Time and again, she stubbornly resisted.

He was beginning to think she was enjoying the spectacle of it all. Eric certainly was, though his wonderment dulled each time he remembered why they were here.

"There you guys are," Jessie called out, waving a teal paw at a couple that clung to one another to avoid falling down. One was a pink tigress in a bikini top, the other a yellow bear with a lolling tongue.

"Hey... hey you..." the bear replied with a wave.

"Scan?" the valet asked them. The tigress removed a glove just long enough to provide a thumbprint.

"Missed you. Thought you might have left without us."

"Naw... couldn't. Couldn't do that."

It wasn't long before the valet was back with a compact hover—a recent model of Sesso Deluxe. He popped the door and hustled out of the way.

"Better let me pilot," Jessie said with a wink to the valet. "You're in no condition."

The valet gave a thumbs-up and mouthed, "Thank you."

"Is... it's a two-seat."

"There's room in the back," Jessie assured the vehicle's owner. "Pile on in. Get cozy." She helped push and squeeze and managed to get both tigress and bear into the cramped back area that irresponsible parents occasionally stuffed their kids into.

Eric pointed at the jumbled mass of fur as he got in via the passenger door Jessie opened for him. "Are they going to be—?"

"Everything's fine," she added hurriedly.

Not quite convinced, Eric settled himself into the non-piloting seat.

When the door didn't close on its own, he gave it a look of mild annoyance. "How do the doors work on this thing?"

Jessie reached across him, but the compact didn't exactly allow convenient access. She gave up, slammed her own door shut, and announced, "Hold on!"

Gunning the engines, Jessie flew them off the ground. The

door mouse-trapped shut, prompting Eric to pull his hand close to his body in self-defense.

"Where's your place?" Jessie asked.

No reply came from the rear seating area.

Eric noticed that his chair was getting bumped from behind. Again. Again. Again. It was like the pendulum of a grandfather clock for regularity. Turning as best he could in his seat, he looked back to see what might be the problem.

"Oh. Sorry. Carry on. They're a little busy back there."

Jessie swooped through traffic but spared a glance back of her own. "For fuck's sake," she muttered. "Never mind. I got this." She tapped a few times on the center console screen, fumbling with the massive fingers of her costume. Eventually, she pulled up a map. A blinky thing moved toward the center, slowly. "Be back at your place in no time at all."

Eric spared another quick look behind him. "Don't think they're in a hurry."

Ten minutes later, Eric sat by as Jessie hauled the lovers out of the back of their own hover.

"You two comin'?" the tigress inquired.

"Sure. Just gonna pop out and grab some wine," Jessie replied without hesitation. This must have been part of her plan.

"We've got wine."

Jessie waved off the idea. "Some stuff you gotta try. We'll be back in under an hour."

"An hour?" the bear asked. Clearly, he was already starting to sober up.

"Yup." Jessie didn't leave room for a prolonged argument. She slung herself into the pilot's seat and they took off. "Phew. All right. Settle in. It's smaller than Earth, but Mars is still pretty big. High atmo, we'll still be a couple hours in the air getting to New Singapore."

She scratched at her wrist.

Eric watched from the corner of his eye.

"The hell?"

Eric looked out the side window, ignoring her.

"What's the deal? We're done with the costumes. Either tell me how to take it off or let the magic run out or whatever."

"I didn't know how the costumes fit. So I just made us into animal-people."

"WHAT?" She pawed at her face. She pulled fur. "Ow! What the hell, Eric!" They drifted out of the traffic flow. Buildings rose up toward them.

"It's undoable. But the hover might not like it."

"Oh, if you weren't my little brother..." she threatened.

Eric giggled.

"You think this is funny?"

He nodded, unable to get words out past his giggles.

After a moment, the infectious nature of laughter kicked in, and Jessie joined him. "Fuck you. Goddammit, Eric. If I land, can you put us back?"

"Sure thing."

The hover angled downward. Jessie parked them in a warehouse loading zone that wasn't open this time of night. Taking long strides, Eric counted out thirty paces and deemed that a safe distance.

With another snap of his fingers, they were back to their old selves.

"That wasn't funny." Jessie's smirk belied her point.

"Very much not," Eric agreed, grinning as he headed back to the hover with her.

Jessie pushed the door shut behind him, then circled around to her side and got in. "C'mon. No more silly shit. We need Esper to help get out of this mess."

Eric nodded his agreement, but he disagreed with her

unspoken assertion that she hadn't needed a little levity right then.

———

Martian airspace grew more dense with traffic the lighter it got outside. Part of circling the red globe was dealing with time zones along the way. Each time the hour rolled back, Eric giggled.

"Quit it. Act like you've been offworld before."

"But being *on*world, I get to see time travel," he countered, pointing to the dashboard chrono. "Even scientists believe time can go backwards."

Jessie covered a yawn with the back of her hand. "If time were really backing up, I'd be getting less tired."

"You should have napped."

"I'm flying."

"Autopilot. That's a thing, right? I'm not making that up?"

If only it were that easy. "Yeah, it's a thing. And if this were a social visit, that might cut it. But we're fugitives. I don't get the luxury of letting autopilot protect us."

Cityscape zoomed past beneath them, closer beneath them than it had been twenty minutes ago. Some pilots liked to stay barely suborbital on long hauls, then corkscrew down when they were above their destination. Jessie preferred the more common cruising lanes, offering a gentler descent and more traffic to disappear amongst.

"Should we comm ahead?"

Jessie muttered under her breath.

"Huh? Didn't catch that."

"I said I would if I remembered her ID."

"Oh." Eric appeared sullen, then perked up. "What if we contact the Rucker Initiative? They must know her comm ID."

If Jessie were Esper, she'd have fired anyone who dared give out her personal comm ID. Anyone who needed it should have already had it. Contingency plans shouldn't have needed to go as deep as "I was time traveling and had to core out my datapad to prevent it being used as evidence against me."

"They probably don't." They'd gotten close enough now for Jessie to steer them out of the long-haul lanes and merge into local traffic patterns for New Singapore. Lucky for her, the city hadn't changed much from the last time she'd been here. Of course, the last time she'd been to Mars, she hadn't been old enough for a pilot's license.

Eric didn't comment. He had his face pressed to the window. Jessie swore he'd have put his head right outside like a dog if the windows opened at this speed. What was the big deal about a core world city anyway? With rare exception, they all looked alike.

Jessie did a flyby of the mansion, not overhead, given a keep-out zone showing on the hover's map, but close enough for a visual. The city had encroached on what had once been an isolated compound set off from the congestion and skyscrapers. It seemed that Esper hadn't been able to resist cashing in on the lucrative hunger of real estate developers.

"Hey! That was it!"

"Glad you're paying attention. But we can't just land a stolen hover on Aunt Esper's lawn."

"She could buy it. Then it wouldn't be stolen."

Jessie shook her head as she searched for a parking zone with space for them. It was coming up on lunchtime in the city, and soon workers on their meal breaks would be clogging the streets. An angry growl in her stomach reminded her that the last thing she'd given it was hard liquor.

There would be time for that later.

Street parking was first come, first serve. Jessie jetted down

Weisan Avenue when a gray Infinisky Z lifted off from outside a karate studio. The pilot of a Pontifex XL had noticed as well and was flying the right direction to get there first.

Jessie slammed open the throttle, briefly overcoming the hover's gravity stabilizer. She was pinned back against her seat. From the corner of her eye, she noticed Eric hadn't been. There was no time to get pissy about wizards ignoring the laws of physics. Quick as she'd accelerated, she braked just as hard, jamming the little hover's poor maneuvering thrusters to max.

The hover fishtailed and swung around, sliding into the space mere meters ahead of the Pontifex. But that victory didn't mean the other pilot was ready to let things go. He pulled up alongside Jessie's stolen Sesso, screaming through two windows and still not able to do better than hand gestures to get his anger across.

Jessie stepped out.

She pounded on the Pontifex pilot's passenger window with the butt of her fist. "Keep moving, capo. Don't try me today."

"Temper."

She turned to spot Eric behind her with his scoldy face on, learned right from Mom. With a flipped finger, she sent the Pontifex on its way.

"Right. Sorry. I'm a little thin right now."

"I found a couple weird Martian coins; let's get you an ice cream."

She didn't bother asking what "found" meant in this context. "Need more than ice cream."

They settled on hot dogs. Jessie wolfed hers down as they made their way to Aunt Esper's place. Eric treated his like a proper meal, going so far as to tuck a napkin into his collar in case of spilled condiments.

"Hope the chef isn't offended that we ate street food before coming over," Eric observed as the gates to the property came into view.

"Least of our problems right now." Security had stepped up in the past five years. Well, the past ten or twelve, however long it had been since she'd last been by here. "Looks like Esper's worried about the state of this planet, too. Let me do the talking."

Guards at the gate were nothing new. Esper had protected her family with private security since taking over the Rucker Initiative. But this was a new level. Even outside the gatehouse, there were black-armored pricks with blaster rifles. Worse, there was a middle-aged man in a skullcap and baggy sleeves. He openly wore a silver pendant, but rather than the C with a bolt of lightning through it, there was an M encircled by a serpent biting its own tail.

"Keep moving," one of the pricks warned.

"Here to see Esper Richelieu."

"Keep moving," the guy repeated, adding a twirling finger gesture in case Jessie couldn't understand the very English she'd spoken back to him.

"She knows us. Put me on camera. It'll take two seconds."

"Candidate Richelieu isn't seeing visitors." This time it was the wizard who spoke.

"Is Auntie Karen home, at least?" Eric interjected, apparently taking the intervention of *their* wizard as his clue to disobey orders and join the discussion.

"Auntie?" the wizard asked with an arched brow.

"Unofficial," Jessie assured the wizard, who clearly outranked the glorified blaster racks. "Old family friends. Please. We're not scrubs looking for table scraps."

The wizard turned to the gatehouse. "Check them out. Bring them to the guest house."

Armed guards surrounded them. "Don't make any sudden

moves," one warned, apparently oblivious to the fact that they were about to gain VIP status and potentially get them fired soon.

"Seriously, I *know* Esper. She doesn't need protection. This is overkill."

When they reached the guest house, Jessie was shocked to find it far from a deserted set of spare rooms for when out-of-town guests stayed over. First off, there were people everywhere. They wore suits and ties, headsets, datagoggles, carried datapads, and talked constantly.

A blonde woman in a gray pantsuit met them at the door. "Volunteers? Ship them over to Watney Arena and get them hats."

At the mention of hats, Jessie spotted a few people wearing reddish-orange ball caps with Esper's name on it. Or rather, the word was Espère with the accent and final E a different hue.

"They're not volunteers."

The blonde woman sized them up. "Lemme guess. Long-lost relatives?"

The guard nodded.

"Family friends," Jessie clarified. "And we're not looking for a handout; we just need to see—"

"She's not here. We're very busy. It's a big day for us. If you can sit quietly in a corner, we'll see about someone helping you after the speech."

"Speech?" Jessie echoed, slow to catch up. She was putting together pieces but didn't have enough of them yet to see the picture. Apparently, Esper was running for office. As a prominent businesswoman and philanthropist, it wasn't the craziest notion in the galaxy.

Someone shouted above the general din of voices, "It's starting!"

A giant holo-projector flickered on, and the conversations

ended. Everyone turned to look. There was Esper, three meters tall in holographic form, towering over the viewers in the guest house foyer. She stood behind a lectern bearing a logo that had once been associated with the Mars First movement.

Five years ago, Mars First had been considered terrorists.

Esper looked the same as ever, statuesque and bright-eyed. She wore her hair in a side flip, held in place by magic or high-tech styling tricks and showing off diamond earrings and matching necklace. If she was campaigning as a working-class candidate, she was missing on tone. Even on holograph, her suit looked expensive. But as soon as she spoke, all thoughts about superficial issues faded.

"My fellow Martians, we stand at the fulcrum of galactic history. Every one of us can trace our roots back to Earth. But long ago, that tree shed its fruit, and the seeds have grown. We stand now as tall and strong as Earth—but healthier. We are healthier because we have cast off the rot that pervades that decrepit third rock orbiting Sol. We are not bound to that corruption any longer, no matter what force the Earthlings may employ to keep us under their boot.

"None will ever forget the bravery and sacrifice of our armed forces. The Admirals' Council saved us at a time when quick action and moral certitude were necessary for the survival of the Martian way of life. We owe them a debt that can never be fully repaid.

"But they were also never elected to lead us. They were not trained to handle civilian administration or set policy for a prosperous future. It's unfair to their heroism that we judge them by these standards. We've known from the beginning

that our current situation would be temporary. I say that now is the time. Now is when we demonstrate that we are more than a moment, more than a refusal to bow to Earth's tyranny. We will return to civilian governance. We will allow the military to resume their vital function of defending the democracy we enjoy.

"*Thus, it is with gratitude and humility that I announce my candidacy for the first president of a free, independent Martian Alliance of Represented Systems.*

"*Thank you.*"

The political staffers and volunteers cheered and applauded, giving a standing ovation for a woman who wasn't even present to appreciate it. While obviously the rest of them had their own agenda, Jessie had been piecing together information to try to explain the current state of Mars.

Some rogue faction, presumably within Earth Navy, had broken Mars away from ARGO and declared martial law. OK. That meant that maybe there would be a sympathetic faction for an Earth Navy deserter out there.

Also, Esper was getting political. Not surprising. As an accomplished wizard, she'd have been ruled out for office on Earth, other than the specific senate seats reserved for the Convocation. But barring that, she was a candidate better able to protect herself from assassination than most.

The most important takeaway from the speech, however, was that Jessie and Eric Ramsey would be a political liability. Troublemakers were a scandal waiting to happen.

Eric was applauding along with the rest of them. Maybe louder. The grin on his face looked genuine. He caught her looking his way "Isn't it great? Auntie Esper's going to be a great president."

Jessie clapped halfheartedly, mostly so as not to stand out.

It wasn't as if she *didn't* support Aunt Esper's political aspirations. Presently, it just seemed a little unlikely that she or her brother was going to be voting.

"All right, you two," the blonde staffer said as she circled back to them. By the grin on her face, maybe they'd find her in a helpful mood. "What's your story?"

"I'm sorry. Who are you, exactly?" Jessie asked.

"That's supposed to be my line. I'm Shelsea Moulin, Deputy Communications Director for the Esper for President campaign. Now, I'll make this blunt... Who the hell are you two? And before I get some bullshit slung my way, just know that we'll be background-checking both of you before you get one rung higher on the ladder than me."

Well, that certainly put a damper on things.

Esper they could deal with. She'd listen. She'd understand. She might get mad at them or be disappointed in their decisions, but she wouldn't turn them over to the authorities.

Unfortunately, these were authorities, and they were planting themselves steadfastly between the Ramseys and Esper.

An underling approached with a thumb scanner.

Eric tugged on Jessie's sleeve. Trying to act casual, she followed his gaze.

"Scan or you can sit tight while Civil Defense comes to pick you up," Shelsea snapped. "I have better things to do than vet charity cases."

Jessie registered the words for later processing. Outside, in Esper's front garden, the non-Convocation wizard was conferring with two figures she'd seen just once before. Not that she needed more than once to form a lasting impression.

Slater and Snow.

Eric's parole officers.

They'd tracked Eric down.

"Sorry to bother you. Maybe we'll get in touch with Esper after the campaign." She grabbed Eric and pushed through the crowd of campaign staff, heading through the foyer away from the front door.

"Hey!" Shelsea shouted after them.

Jessie didn't turn back. "We'll show ourselves out! We've been here before!"

Jessie burst out the back door of Esper's guest house, leaving a wake of offended political operatives aghast and ineffectual behind her.

"Sorry. Excuse us. Congratulations. Sorry. Esper for President," Eric patched hurt feelings as he kept up gamely.

The side garden of the Richelieu Estate opened into a hedge maze, three meters high and meticulously manicured. Jessie raced straight for the entrance. In her head, she fought to remember the layout, not just of the property but of the maze in particular.

Swift afoot, she reached the maze after opening up a sizable lead over her brother, who ran like he'd only seen it done in holovids, pumping his arms in exaggerated motions that didn't really help the process. Hot on his heels, armed security closed in. Two of them. Burly and menacing. They could break Eric just tackling him.

"Go go go!" Eric shouted as he panted for breath. "Left, left, right, straight, left, right, right, straight. GO!"

Jessie didn't even process the full list, presumably of the directions through the maze.

That was when Jessie remembered that this was, in the grand scheme of things, amateur hour. They hadn't frisked her. She still had a blaster. There were ways to ditch a weapon discreetly, even while being pretty closely observed. But part of her training had taught her never to disarm herself unless absolutely necessary.

In one smooth motion, she drew her stolen blaster, flipped to stun, and squeezed off a warning shot.

Even seeing the blue fuzz of neurodisruptive plasma sailing past, the guards diverted to cover like she was manning a megawatt plasma turret.

Before they realized that they were taking cover from someone whom they had outnumbered and outgunned, Eric reached the entrance of the maze.

"What were those directions?" Jessie demanded.

"Just follow me." Eric set off at a huffing, puffing, leisurely pace. Jessie didn't press the issue, knowing that athletics weren't his forte, but she kept an eye behind them, watching for signs their pursuers had gotten brave.

The maze was meant as a whimsical wonderland. It was a place for kids to play and Esper and Karen to steal a little privacy. The paths were granite, marked with bronze medallions, no two alike but also not particularly helpful unless you memorized them all. Eric didn't even glance down at them as he navigated them without hesitation. As he caught his breath, their pace sped up.

"Glad you remember the way."

"I have a pretty good memory."

"You forget my birthday every year."

Eric took a pair of turns, getting ahead of her momentarily. He waited until she had a direct line to hear him before continuing. "Good memory. Bad with calendars." He pointed around the next corner. "This is the edge of the estate. We can get out here."

When Jessie came around, she saw a part of the maze she'd swear she had never explored. It wasn't like they'd spent *that* much time here as kids. Just occasional visits when the *Mobius* stopped by Mars. Maybe Eric had come by again with Mom and Dad after she'd left for boot camp.

A line of apple trees reached right up to the security perimeter. As climbing went, it was hard to get much easier than an apple tree.

"Up and over," she told herself. There was no time for detailed planning. New Singapore was massive. Get out into the city, and she'd test her urban survival training against the local police any day.

The first branch was a tall step. The next a quick grab of the trunk and a hop. She climbed without hesitation, knowing that the perfect was the enemy of the good enough. Once at the top of the wall, she'd coach Eric on the ascent. Even as clumsy and awkward as her brother might be, he should have had no trouble managing the climb.

"FREEZE!" a voice boomed just as she set foot on the wall.

"Shit! Eric, quick, get up here!" She scanned the ground below the tree. Nothing. She checked the trees to either side of her in case he'd tried a parallel course. Still nothing.

"Why?" Eric replied. "You should come down here."

Jessie whipped around only to find her brother waving up at her from the outside of the wall.

It was a four-meter fall. Jessie dropped down, grabbing the top and arresting her momentum briefly, then falling into a roll to cushion her landing at the bottom.

"How did you—?" She stopped the question. "Forget it. Magic. C'mon. Let's move."

Jessie led the way, focusing on putting as much distance as possible between them and Aunt Esper's place without drawing undue attention to themselves. Side streets. Pedestrian malls. Cutting through counter service restaurants.

One thing nagged at her as Jessie's mind spun down from

pure survival mode. "Once this blows over, we should warn Esper about putting up some magic defenses around the house. Pretty slipshod. If she's gonna be a big deal—well, a *political* big deal—she should up the security."

"Nothing wrong with her security."

Jessie glared back, but this was no time to get into one of Eric's nonsense, nitpicky, magic-babble arguments. She let the matter drop. They still hadn't found either shelter, aid, or a way off Mars, and that fuel leak had caught fire.avbgk

---

"I hate Mars," Jessie declared.

Overhead, Civil Defense hovers patrolled, blaring over their loudspeakers. *"Attention, citizens, be on the lookout for two fugitives, one male, one female. Considered armed and extremely dangerous."*

Peering up from beneath an Espère ball cap, Jessie watched the patrol until it passed behind the skyscrapers before she lowered the arm, keeping Eric from stepping into view. This was the fourth time the CDP had done a flyby. Stay on the streets long enough, someone was going to finger Jessie as acting suspicious when the authorities floated past.

"Maybe you shouldn't have shot at them," Eric pointed out, adopting the same private-in-a-public-setting tone she'd used to complain about the red planet.

"This isn't the time."

"You can say that again."

Jessie snorted in amusement despite herself. It was either accept the absurdity of their situation or go nuts. Tired, hungry, and desperate, nothing would have pleased her more than collapsing in exhaustion, only to wake up and find it had all been an elaborate prank.

She'd still kill Eric, but it would be a relief.

"Go, Esper!" someone called out from down the street as they approached. Jessie raised a hand in acknowledgment. It was better than wearing Earth Navy gear and better than leaving clear sight lines to aerial surveillance, but the hat was drawing more attention than she would have preferred.

"Our luck is leaking."

"Huh?"

Jessie turned to see someone among the pedestrian masses conversing in animated fashion with a pair of city police. A finger pointed in their direction. Jessie averted her eyes to avoid being identified immediately.

"Right at the next block."

"But that's—"

"Just do it."

There was no time for long-term thinking. Whatever objection Eric might have been trying to voice, there was a ninety percent chance it was nonsense and a twenty percent chance it was irrelevant. Unless the middle of New Singapore had an open pit construction site or there was a squad of soldiers lined up with blaster rifles trained on the intersection, there was no reason to avoid evasive maneuvering.

Afternoon had waned into evening. New Singaporeans looking for dinner and maybe a little fun on a night out had all apparently congregated on this one street, wider than most and blocked off from terrestrial traffic. An archway stretching across the street declared it Cloudview Plaza. Buildings and expanses of open air had kept the music from spilling over into the main travel roads. Now, it encompassed them.

Eric shouted to be heard. "When you see people leaving with food on sticks, you know there's a street fair." He glanced quickly toward the crowd and back again to his sister. "This was bigger than I was expecting."

Even amid the revelry, Jessie saw signs of trouble. The New Singaporeans were a mix of just-off-the-chrono office workers and partiers who'd been home to change. Armor-clad officers stood out like black olives on pizza.

"Duck a little. Keep moving. Don't get separated." Jessie took her own advice and grabbed Eric by the hand for good measure. While not physically imposing, she had the very military habit of perfect posture. It took a conscious effort to slouch and crouch and slink her way through the masses.

Along the way, she ditched her hat. In these close quarters, bumping into strangers was common. She picked up a bracelet, some cufflinks, and a few terras' worth of Martian hardcoin that felt weird between her fingers. Bribes and fences were in their future in the best of cases. In the worst, they were going to get sent up for a lot worse than pickpocketing should those police get hold of them.

"In there!" Eric suggested, giving a tug on the hand Jessie clutched. With his other hand, he directed her attention to a nightclub of sorts. It had an American West theme and coughed bouncy, twangy, drawling music into the plaza.

What Jessie saw was a venue where a ten-gallon hat might not look out of place called the A-okay Corral.

"Yeah. Go. I'm right behind you." With that, Jessie relinquished her grip and took up a rearguard position, watching for signs that anyone was taking special note of their route. If things went smoothly, there were worse places to wait out a shitstorm than a cowboy bar that emanated an aroma of beer and steak as they entered.

One final look over her shoulder confirmed her worst fears. Not only had she failed to spot their pursuit until they were a dozen meters away, they shouted into a comm piece when they made eye contact.

"Table or bar?" a hostess inquired. She was thirty-something with auburn pigtails dangling from beneath a cowgirl hat. Her 'period accent' sounded like she'd failed acting school.

"Table," Eric answered thoughtfully. "Something dance floor–adjacent if you've got it."

"Actually, where are your washrooms?" Jessie amended hurriedly.

Their hostess pointed. "Right thatta way."

Eric fell in behind her as Jessie made rude haste through diners and waitstaff.

But at the far end of the establishment, more uniformed officers were pouring in. Looking behind them, Jessie realized their initial pursuers were already inside. The hostess pointed the same direction she'd just directed the Ramsey siblings.

As Jessie reached for the blaster tucked in the back of her waistband, Eric caught her wrist. "Let's dance." She tried to voice an objection, but his timing in cutting her off was impeccable. "Trust me."

The dance floor was the central hub of the A-okay Corral and seemed to be the main draw. Tiles glowed in a slow-shifting pattern of hues that spanned the range of a desert sunset. Atop those tiles, an all-ages crowd had arrayed themselves into an informal grid, performing a sequence of dance moves timed to the music. Everyone appeared to know the dance, and the synchronization was pretty good for an amateur performance.

Eric stepped into a spot at the periphery of the grid and joined in.

Step, step, clap. Sidestep. Slide step. Clap. Hop, hop. Turn, turn.

And the process resumed in the opposite direction.

Eric had two left feet, and neither of them could dance. But he bumbled along without anyone complaining, even as he jostled and elbowed people when he messed up.

Jessie hesitated. Eric jerked his head for her to join him. The police were going table to table. More appeared at the door and the rear of the club. The odds of them missing Jessie and Eric just because they'd joined the dance seemed slim.

But Jessie felt her toe tapping to the music. She clapped when the dancers clapped. Soon, she was there beside Eric, flubbing her way through the routine. None of it was difficult, however, and soon both were just part of the show.

Another song started without a break. A couple dancers snuck away. Others joined in. A new dance began, and everyone else seemed to know it already.

Forward. Clap. Backward. Clap. Slide step right. Half turn. Overhead clap.

Jessie picked up on it quickly. In fact, she barely felt like she was dancing at all. The moves fit the music so perfectly; she just did what came naturally. At her side, Eric appeared lost in a trance, moving flawlessly in time with everyone else.

The song lasted for hours, it felt.

Jessie blinked away a daydream when Eric's fingers snapped in front of her eyes.

"C'mon. Let's go."

It took a moment for Jessie to get her bearings. The music had changed, but the dance kept going without a pause. And while it had been busy on the dance floor before, now it was packed shoulder to shoulder.

Uniformed officers danced in perfect harmony with the bar patrons.

Jessie had to watch her step to avoid tripping over discarded blaster rifles as Eric led the way toward the rear exit of the A-okay Corral.

Outside, Eric was shimmying a little and humming along

with the latest song, even as a final closing of a door blocked them from hearing it any longer.

"Eric, what did you do?"

"Yes, Eric," a familiar voice called out. "Just what did you do in there?"

Snow and Slater had found them.

Eric's shoulders fell. "Apparently, I was leading you right to us."

"Eric, I'm going to need you to come along quietly. No one wants an incident, right?" Wizard Snow's tone of voice resembled that of a zookeeper approaching a wild beast. He crept forward, hands in plain sight.

"I don't want to go," Eric said with a tiny shake of his head.

Wizard Slater circled around the side, slowly closing off a potential escape back into the A-okay Corral. "You knew this would happen. You broke our agreement."

"Only a little."

Wizard Snow appeared to be in no hurry now that he had Eric engaged. Jessie knew that if she didn't do something, they were going to get close enough to grab him. Her problem was she didn't have clue one how to stop a wizard who saw her coming.

If Eric was half as dangerous as they treated him, she might have some chance of swinging the balance.

But... Eric.

Eric was the kid who ran from fights. The kid who stopped to pat strangers' dogs. The kid who drew with Wax-i-Rods until he was twelve.

"Time travel is never little," Snow scolded gently. "Now, I don't think anyone wants to get hurt today."

Eric stepped in front of Jessie. "This is just about me(run). We don't need to get my(run)sister involved(run)." The asides were in Kejathi, the only non-human language Jessie spoke worth a damn. Shoni had insisted her kids learn it, and being cooped up on the same ship, she'd absorbed the basics.

"What was that?" Slater asked. "Are you trying to signal your sister? No tricks, Eric."

"I don't want trouble. I just want to go. And she's being a little dense right now."

Jessie scowled. "I'm not ditching you."

Eric sighed. "I'm really sorry about this."

He clapped his hands. Mars rocked beneath Jessie's feet. Smoke exploded all around. Every light chasing away the darkness went out at once.

A hand grabbed hers.

Coughing, Jessie allowed herself to be towed out of the blast zone.

"What... happened?"

"Less talking. More running away." Eric let go of her hand and allowed Jessie to take the lead.

As if she had a plan.

But moving *was* the plan. Fear was a better vise tightening around the adrenal gland than anger or duty ever could be. Those two punch-clock wizards wouldn't dare risk matching the Ramseys' heedless, headlong rush through the New Singapore night.

━━

"You need to pay better attention," were Eric's first words once they felt safe enough to stop running. They strolled past the glass-fronted window of an all-night fitness center. Night owl

Martians ran laps and rowed imaginary boats without going anywhere.

Jessie's eyes were drawn to the buff figures in tight workout gear, which she used as cover to peer over her shoulder for signs of anyone tailing them. So far, the coast was clear. Unfortunately, with wizards after them, she didn't know how much she could expect to see them coming.

"I wasn't going to leave you behind."

"It's called a head start. A diversion I was going to use to make the bigger diversion."

Jessie rolled her eyes, certain Eric couldn't see them. "That was plenty of diversion without my help."

"It could have been smaller. Someone could have gotten hurt."

It was the first time the potential for casualties from the incident behind the A-okay Corral entered her mind. "We're doing what we have to. We just need to catch a break. And the best way to catch a break is—" She paused, drawing out the last syllable as a prompt.

"To make it yourself," Eric finished dutifully. Then, suddenly, he brightened. "I've got it!"

"Got what?" Jessie watched more intently through the fitness center windows. The workout warriors came and went through a door in the rear corner, near a main desk.

"We hide at my apartment."

Despite herself, Jessie burst out laughing.

"What? It's the last place they'd look."

Shit. He'd been serious. "Where do I start? Maybe the fact that 'the last place they'd look' is Hollyworld bullshit. Anytime someone says that, it turns out to be a mistake. If they haven't figured out who we are yet and staked out your old place they're idiots."

"Right. Old place. Doesn't seem like it should be that old.

Maybe the Convocation kept up the rent, and everything's just the way I left it but dustier."

"More likely they've—hey, watch it, pal!" Jessie snapped as a pedestrian brushed against her. She instinctively checked for her stolen valuables and her blaster, but the guy hadn't tried to pickpocket her. Once he'd moved along, she continued. "Odds are, they've either cordoned the place off as a crime scene the past five years, or someone else lives there now."

"Unsporting..."

"Hope you weren't attached to anything you left there: clothes, keepsakes, the year 2586..."

Eric gazed through the glass with her. "Amazing the magic going on in there. Scientists *can* manage when they try."

"Come off it. That's physiology at work."

"Run around, lift heavy things, you get fit," Eric stated, drawing an indifferent shrug for explaining the obvious. "But none of them are running anywhere, lifting anything. They're flailing around on crazy machines, and because they *believe* that it makes them fit, it works!"

"We're going in and ask about a membership. I'm Glacy—"

"Is that Tracy with a G or Gracie with an L?"

"It doesn't matter. And you're my fiancé Jelvin."

"I've always fancied myself more of a silent-D Derek."

"Just... be Jelvin."

Eric rolled his eyes melodramatically in what Jessie assumed had to be a mockery of her mannerism. "Fiiiine. But next time, I get to pick names."

Just as she was about to point out that this was a one-time proposition, she realized it might not be. They were stranded, the only two people in the galaxy who hadn't aged in the past five years, and the prospects of getting back to their own time seemed remote. "Yeah. Whatever. Now play along."

"What's the plan?"

Thankfully, Eric was being remarkably sanguine about their plight. All of it, right from the discovery of their mishap. If she could keep him going without a meltdown, maybe they could get out of this after all.

"We pretend we want to sign up. Get a tour. Snag new clothes from the lockers when no one's looking."

"But aren't lockers... locked?"

Jessie fixed him with a Mom look. "Really? You're telling me you can't pop a simple digital lock? What happened to 'locks don't apply to wizards'?"

She'd never expected an actual blush, but she got one out of her brother. "I never knew you heard that."

"I *always* eavesdropped when Mom chewed you out. And spare me the 'robbing innocent people' bit," she added, keeping her voice down. "They can afford a membership to avoid walking and manual labor. They can afford a couple new outfits."

Without waiting for the Wishy Washy Commission to comment further, Jessie headed inside.

Due to the design of the place, their tour started before they talked to a soul. Lines of Stretchercise machines lined the walkway to one side, while to the other, electro-grav dumbbells provided a pantomime-looking workout to the practitioner of the strength-gaining arts.

With the eye of someone on the fence about joining, Jessie took in the sights without pausing on her way to the sales desk. The saleswoman on staff had skin that had been exfoliated with an industrial floor buffer and a smile that was backlit in golden light by some kind of body mod.

"Welcome to Blasters. New members?" She had a voice like a kiosk set to perma-perky. The nametag on her red uniform sports bra read "Alex."

Jessie's first instinct was to comment on how non-Martian a

name she had. Icebreakers like that put people at ease under normal circumstances. But given the politics she'd seen so far, any implication that she wasn't Martian enough might come across as poli-aggressive.

"Thinking about it," Jessie replied noncommittally. "Mind showing us around?"

"Sure. Can I get your names?"

"Glacy McCray," Jessie answered without a hitch. "Soon to be Glacy Evans. This is my fiancé."

"Jelvin," Eric came in on cue with a wan smile and a timid wave.

Alex tapped their names into a datapad as she walked. "Super. What are your fitness goals?"

Jessie thought on the fly, not having ever signed up for a gym membership before. "Well, I just got a new office job, and I was hoping for someplace I could pop in on my way home. Fry some myofibrils. Cycle electrolytes through my system." She hooked a thumb at Eric. "He's a work in progress."

"Promoted to a planetside post?" Alex asked with a smirk.

Jessie's guts clenched. Shit. How the hell did civilians talk? "I wasn't angling for a discount."

"Knew it. It's just an aura. My Keven has it, too. He's in Mars Marine Corps." She pumped a fist and gave a lighthearted "oorah."

After the initial small talk, Jessie let Alex show them around. The equipment and facilities *were* on the impressive side. If Jessie really had been in the market for a place to avoid working out on base, she'd have considered it. But eventually, Alex led them to where they really needed to be.

"And these are our changing rooms. Private shower stalls and changing booths. Thumb-scan lockers."

Jessie made a show of looking everything over like a building inspector. Little "ahs" and "hmms" kept Alex from cutting short her evaluation. When she found their guide's attention wandering, she made eye contact with Eric.

Now. Do it.

If her brother could read eyes, that was the message he was meant to take away.

A moment later, trusting in her brother to take care of his own shit, she got her answer. "Hey, what are you doing in there?"

"Me?" Eric replied with guilty haste. "Nothing."

"That was locked." An irate weightlifter got in Eric's face. "Alex, your new fish is a klepto."

"I'm really sorry. If I—"

"Shut up," Jessie snapped. There was no time for de-escalation. She had her blaster out and trained on the sweaty fitness freak before anyone else reacted. When Alex twitched toward the door, Jessie quickly switched targets. "Hands up, both of you."

All three lifted their hands, including Eric, who'd been plundering the locker for shirts and still held onto a garment.

"Not you." Eric put his arms down.

Alex flashed a terrified smile. "Listen. I don't know if it's drugs or—"

"No talking. Close and lock the door." Jessie waggled the blaster barrel to coax Alex along. The saleswoman hurriedly did as she was told. The door beeped as she sealed them in. To Eric, she snapped, "What's the idea? Getting spotted *and* picking a guy twice your size?" She held her free hand out to the brawny wall of a man who'd come to change into the very clothes her brother was considering.

But Eric had a ready answer. "Well, I was thinking a floppy-boy look. Rolled sleeves and pant legs. Punch an extra hole in this spiffy manual belt." He wiggled the prong on the traditionalist waist cinch. "I was hoping for a hat, but I can make do without."

Fuming, but reluctantly admitting his plan held merit, Jessie kept their impromptu backup plan moving. "Pop lockers until you find something for me."

"Look. If you're looking for marbits, I can—"

Jessie cut Alex off with a reaiming of her blaster at the woman's forehead. "I said shut the fuck up."

Without looking up from the row of lockers he was forcing open as quick as if the locks didn't exist, Eric chimed in. "Quit pretending you might shoot them over some spare clothes."

When the big guy took that as a cue to step forward, Eric looked up from his work.

A barrier of wireframe purple runes sprang up between Jessie and the potential for a messy confrontation. "Don't pretend *she's* the dangerous one here." He tossed an outfit at Jessie one piece at a time, including shoes that looked to be her size. "Now, are the two of you going to voluntarily forget that you ever saw us or anything that happened back here?

"Or would you like... help?"

"We saw nothing."

"Yeah. Nothing."

Jessie and Eric quickly changed clothes.

He left the fitness center looking, as promised, like many of the slovenly youths of Mars with their comically oversized outfits. She looked more like his mother than a sister two years older. Walking stiffly on high heels she hadn't tried on since pre-enlistment days, she shuffled down the street like she'd come from a ceremony for the Boringest Business of the Year award, completed with late-model datagoggles she didn't dare turn on until she could disable the location tracking.

Once they were alone in the city, she caught Eric grinning.

"You sounded like you meant business back there."

"Thanks. It's fun playing the bad guy if no one calls your bluff. I wasn't going to erase their memories."

"These clothes fit shockingly well. Did you magic them?"

Eric giggled. "There's no Order of Armani. Otherwise, I'd have made up a hat to go with this look. No, I just spotted a woman on a Stretchercise machine that looked your size and opened lockers until I found hers."

"Nice work."

If Eric could keep up this level of usefulness, maybe they weren't completely fucked after all.

"We're being followed," Eric stated nonchalantly.

Jessie directed them to a right turn at the next intersection and used the motion to spare a glance back. "I don't have them."

"I can feel them," Eric insisted.

Mars had been relentless. New Singapore didn't sleep; it barely yawned. Streets were scattered with people at every hour of the clock. Patrols roved the skies, and the Ramseys weren't the only ones who shied from those menacing gazes from on high. Lodgings required ID. Restaurants demanded digital payments. They'd been surviving on street food and public washrooms.

If Jessie were in charge of the manhunt, she'd have had people watching the housing shelters and charity pantries. She had to assume that the Martian authorities weren't idiots.

Eric, thus far, had been little help. At best, he got them out of snags he'd gotten them into, like the fitness center, but mostly he vacillated between useless and actively distracting.

"This better not be another sasquatch-under-the-bed."

"Just because we've dodged them twice without you seeing anything doesn't mean they weren't real."

This was the trouble with wizards. It was damn near impossible to tell whether they were savants or scammers. Only Eric's utter failure to turn out like her and Mom kept Jessie from assuming her brother had an angle here.

"Which way?"

Eric hesitated. "Left. Behind us. Right."

"They're boxing us in..." Jessie didn't need to guess. This was standard for capturing elusive targets. Leave one escape route. That's where the trap would lie, hidden better than the beaters who shook the bushes to spur them along.

"I have a thought."

Jessie didn't have time for his idle musings right now, and that had definitely sounded like his idle musing voice just now. "Do you know anyone in the Martian underworld?"

"There *are* no more Martian syndicates. Not since Esper negotiated the Great Amnesty."

Jessie scoffed as she hurried her pace, unable to explain even to herself why she'd want to reach the trap any faster, but slowing down only meant the embarrassing fate of being apprehended by the distraction. "If you don't know anyone, fine. Just don't be sucker enough to believe crime's gone."

"It's been five extra years. Besides, I have an alternate solution." He slowed his pace.

Jessie couldn't afford to let them get separated. She eased up, too. "We need to pick a place to risk a breakthrough. Get indoors. Somewhere with multiple exits. Hopefully, we can slip through the net they're spreading for us. With any luck, they won't catch on until we get to lay ions."

"But..."

"C'mon. MOVE."

"Ahem!" Eric cleared his throat dramatically. He pointed. Jessie followed his finger.

The Basilica of St. Ishmael the Spacefarer. The One Church. It was certainly an idea.

From the corner of her eye, under the glow of New Singapore's streetlights, Jessie spotted the uniforms. A CDP patrol ship rounded one of the nearby buildings, providing close air support. If Eric sensed wizards, too, this was a multi-disciplinary strike force cutting them off on all sides.

"Fuck me." Jessie raced up the granite steps toward the church entrance.

"They don't like that kind of language," Eric pointed out.

"Getting it out of my system before we get inside."

―――

The doors stood wide. Big, swinging, wooden, carved, stained and polished and heavy. They exuded age. For a man stranded in his own future, crossing the threshold transported Eric Ramsey back in time.

Incense and wood polish created an aroma found nowhere else. Sonorous notes from a pipe organ sketched out the skeleton of a malformed hymn, discordant and repetitive, as an amateur practiced. Row upon row of wooden pews stood sparsely attended as parishioners prayed or quietly conversed or—in a couple cases —curled up and slept. Candlelight disguised the pervasive glow of science keeping people from tripping over themselves.

As Eric absorbed all this, the doors thundered shut behind them. He whirled to see Jessie fetching a disused beam from its ceremonial place propped against a nearby wall and hefting it into place barring the entrance.

"What is the meaning of this?" a priest in One Church

daily wear demanded, striding down the center aisle. He was of average height, with a long, thin face and a mop of sandy hair cut in the style of a parent with a pair of kitchen shears.

Jessie matched his pace on an intercept course. "You in charge here?"

Unaccustomed to being challenged, the priest blinked as he pulled up short. "No. I'm." He cleared his throat. "I am Father Ranier. And I am *presently* the ranking priest on site. Unbar the gates to this house of the Lord immediately."

"Sanctuary," Eric blurted. Mars was more religious than Earth—or had been five years ago—and had legal protections in place that had expired on the cradle planet centuries ago. He switched to Latin, since the priest looked fresh enough from seminary to still be fluent. "I formally request the protection of the One Church."

The priest's expression shifted once more, this time showing stage fright jitters. "Um. I'm not sure I—that is to say— are you baptized?"

"Shouldn't matter," Eric replied.

"Bat mitzvahed," Jessie added under her breath.

The priest, for some reason, seemed relieved. "Oh. Quite right. Forget I said anything of the sort. Please. Tell me. What sort of trouble are you in?"

Eric looked to Jessie. She had the same question in her eyes. Her shrug was permission to explain their plight as best he could.

Then, just as he was about to launch into a twisted tale of accidental time travel, arcano-administrative sanctions, and incidental pre-war naval desertion, Jessie's eyes went wide. Maybe she had realized how that might sound. A second earlier, he'd taken that shrug as acceptance that they'd have to get into both the nitty and gritty of their predicament.

"We're Earthlings," Jessie cut in. "We booked passage on a

borderlands transport that claimed to be able to get us home. Instead, they dumped us here."

Thunderous pounding drew the attention of everyone inside to the doors. *"Open up. This is Civil Defense."*

Jessie fixed a puppy dog look on the priest. It had always worked on Dad, never on Mom. Eric threw his guess that Father Ranier was more of a Dad. Heck, it was right in his title.

Swallowing back his trepidation, Father Ranier took a fortifying breath and marched up to the door. "This is a house of God. The Martian Independence Charter grants the One Church sovereignty within these walls."

The voice on the other side of the door didn't give up so easily. *"We're not fooling around out here. You have two dangerous fugitives inside. Let us do our jobs. We're protecting you as Martian citizens."*

Growing bold, Father Ranier stood tall as he addressed the door. "I will not violate my holy vows. I have granted sanctuary and accept the risks. If you wish to enter, you must wait for Cardinal Messier to return."

As he turned his back and returned to tending the needs of his flock, Father Ranier lowered his voice. "Do not make me regret my decision. Pray. Make your peace. If you wish to confess, I can guide you through the process."

Eric brightened at the idea. "Oh, I've read all—" An elbow to the ribs cut him short.

"Thank you, Father. I think, for now, a moment of peace will do."

Eric waited for the priest to depart before scolding his sister. "Well, there goes my one thing to do while we're here."

Jessie kept her voice low. "Just don't get any ideas about magic. You look like some sloppy, trendy kid. Don't let on otherwise—get those hands out of your sleeves! Jesus Christ, don't you know how to act in a church?"

Dutifully, Eric removed his hands from the ample sleeves of a man with forearms the size of his thighs. Unable to resist, he bit his lip and held up a finger as if in thought, then answered in the manner of a quiz game contestant. "Um, what are... 'words that don't appear in the Bible'?"

The backhanded slap that followed was well deserved. Eric snickered as he followed Jessie to an empty pew—which stood in plenty.

"What now?" Eric asked. He was legitimately out of ideas. Everything involved magic. Especially anything fun. They could ill afford to get chatty with the congregation; none of their story would stand long under close scrutiny. Short of an impromptu conversion, there was no religious activity in which he could partake. "Would it be considered rude to ask around for a deck of cards?"

"We're not here for R & R. Well, maybe a little rest. But no relaxing. We're in deep shit. You try asking around for what passes for charity chow around here. I'll scout for hidden exits under the pretense of fascination with the architecture. On the off chance there are old sewers under this place, you willing to get that kind of dirty?"

What a question to ask. A sewer was literally the worst of everything people didn't want in their houses and businesses. In the days before waste reclaims, it was one chute fits all—and Mars was *old*. Yellow and brown washroom flushes, toothsoap mixed with saliva, liquor-soaked vomit, rotted food scraps too inedible to compost, Eric pictured himself crawling on his belly through a slurry of it all. Cooped up in a reeking pipe, unable to draw a breath of fresh air. Splashing under half a city before emerging with his borrowed clothes pasted to his body by the filth.

How else could he answer?

"Yeah. Considering what they've got in store for me, there's really no other choice."

◻━━◻

Presidential candidate Esper Richelieu daubed at the corners of her lips with a white cloth napkin, which she then set beside her empty plate and its remnant smears of pancake syrup. When she stood, the assembled donors stood as well. Her departure from the table marked the end of the official part of the event. She'd endured the glad-handing, the schmoozing, the well-wishes mixed with implied requests for favors, the toasts, the well-rehearsed "off the cuff" speeches, and the small talk as everyone ate.

Now, as the function room at the Breton Arms cleared out, Esper was taken into custody by her own staff.

Lacey breezed up like a taxi merging onto Esper's lane on the skyway. She had a datapad and goggles so omnipresent that Esper couldn't picture her without them. Even the color of her eyes remained a mystery. They appeared green, but that was probably just a trick of the light coming from the interior displays. "Overnight polling shows tracking up twelve points after yesterday's announcement."

Esper didn't break stride to carry on the conversation. "To be fair, I wasn't officially a candidate until yesterday. Don't read too much into it."

Stan spoke from her other side, though there had been no sign of his arrival. He'd just suddenly been there all along. "Got you on a pre-noon recording of Mars Tonight."

"Am I on first?"

Stan shook his head. "They have Milady Milanie dropping from a sit-down interview straight into an in-studio set. Then you."

They exited the building. A cordon kept onlookers at bay, leaving an unobstructed path to a limousine.

"You've got me following my daughter's favorite singer?" She didn't feel the need to specify that it was Autumn she referred to; her staff knew. "I'll be lucky to win the ratings battle in my own living room. Lean on her staff to shuffle me to tomorrow."

"Candidate, a word?" a voice snagged her just as Esper reached the door as a junior staffer held it for her. It was Shelsea.

There was no time to dawdle. "With me." Esper tilted her head, indicating the trailing vehicles in their little convoy. "Rest of you, we'll reconvene later."

Esper ducked inside, and Shelsea joined her. When her communications department approached her with that tone of voice, she knew there was PR trouble on the horizon. The door thudded shut. A privacy screen slid closed, isolating them from the pilot.

Shelsea waited. As soon as they were by themselves, she took a breath. "There's a development."

"Please. I'm a big girl. Just set the table, and we'll choke it down."

"There were two individuals who showed up at your house yesterday."

Esper felt her stomach knot. She knew all along that this campaign would paint a target on her; that never bothered her. But smaller targets would mark her whole family. "Was Karen home?"

"No. The old house on Hellas Lake. They claimed to know you."

"Did they? Who wouldn't know we moved?"

Shelsea offered a sympathetic smile. "I know, right? It was

right before the speech, so we back-seated them until we had
two breaths to spare to vet them."

"Who were they?"

"They didn't give names before they laid ions right at the
end of the speech, just as the pundits were coming on to
evaluate you like a high school debater."

"You're evading again. Who were they?"

"Sorry, ma'am. They've been on the local newsfeeds. One
of them took a couple stun blasts at our security people.
They've been on the run from CDP and the Martian Circle
ever since. Now they're holed up in St. Ishmael's, claiming
sanctuary."

"Names. Now." She could tell Shelsea was withholding. If
they were any of her kids' friends, there was going to be hell
to pay.

"It's speculation right now, but CDP seems to think they're
Jessie and Eric Ramsey."

If Esper had been piloting, they'd have crashed on the spot—
even beyond the fact she hadn't flown her own ship in decades. It
had been five years since the accident. She'd kept a thread of hope
alive but realistically never expected to hear from either ever again.
Now, not only were they back, they were in trouble with laws and
factions that didn't even exist when they'd last been on Mars.

"Fuck."

"I brought this to you because you need to keep your cool
when the media brings it up. You can't lose your shit on live
holo."

"Cardinal Messier was just at that breakfast. Get him on a
comm right now. I'll negotiate custody of both of them."

Shelsea wagged a datapad at her. Esper suspected that if
she weren't the boss, her deputy communications director
would have bonked her on the nose with it as a scolding. "This

is why we're having this conversation in a hover. You need to distance yourself from your Ramsey problem. The fewer dots that connect you to that family, the better."

"But they were declared dead. There's got to be some legal loophole we can—"

Shelsea had dropped her datapad to put fingers in both ears. "La la la. I can't hear you trying to subvert laws you're running for office to uphold."

"Fine," Esper replied as she slumped in her seat. She knew Shelsea was still listening. "Point taken."

"We need messaging around conciliation, patience with the process, and allowing the proper authorities to handle this. If they get to you while the Ramseys are still on the street, you need to call for them to turn themselves in."

"Turn themselves in for what?" Esper demanded. "There was a temporal accident. The Convocation confirmed that."

"Don't refer to the Big C as an authority on anything, not even the sun in the sky. We have one special operative of Earth Navy, one Convocation wizard. On the loose. With ties to your family. This isn't a good look. You need them in custody. Maybe back-channel something with Earth to get rid of them. Prisoner exchange or some shit. Not that Admiral Alphonze is likely to make life easy for you without a fight."

Esper shook her head slightly. "I don't envy the machinations you have to consider."

"You won't have to. Either you learn to keep up, or you lose."

Sulking was a bad look, but in the privacy of the limo, Esper pouted for show at least. "I can't let this go."

"You have to."

"They're family."

As Mars raced by outside, Shelsea rubbed her temples. "They're not. Not to the public, at least. They are tertiary players in a redemption story. They are children of criminals you used to associate with. We're already prepping for reactions to the inevitable replaying of footage from you attending that damned memorial service."

Despite the political fallout, Esper couldn't bring herself to regret offering her condolences in person. Even if everyone said they hoped Jessie and Eric would show up again someday, how many of them had believed it?

And what now?

Could Esper really sit by and do nothing just because her lackeys said it was the smart play? Since when had she ever let the smart play, the legal play, the safe play get in the way of doing the *right* thing?

"We're helping them. Hand me your datapad."

Maliciously complying, Shelsea turned over the device.

Esper immediately handed it back. "Turn it on."

"No."

"I'm sorry. Who works for whom here?"

"There is zero job security working on a ship where the captain's burning holes through the hull." Esper could see the frustration, the conflict, the indecision as Shelsea paused. "If we're going to do this, it has to be through intermediaries."

"Progress. Keep talking."

"This isn't my area of expertise."

"How many people do you need?"

Shelsea frowned thoughtfully. "We're stretched a little thin right now. If I pulled in—"

"Not campaign staff. My people."

"Excuse me?" Shelsea's eyes widened.

"This isn't PR. This is off the books. I have people for this. Take a personal day. A week. Whatever it takes. Show up at the main house. Back entrance. Sit on the stairs. Whoever finds you, ask for Brenda."

"Who's Brenda?"

"What a wonderful question. She's no one. Doesn't exist. But the household staff knows the code word. They'll get you in touch with real help."

"Define 'real.'"

Esper gave her best cryptic smile. "The Rucker Initiative didn't start out as a charity."

⸺

Cardinal Dustin Messier exited the washroom, still adjusting his cassock. Father Flores met him with an "I have something to say, but I'm worried about decorum" look in his eyes. With a plate of too-greasy breakfast sausage and two cups of black coffee still gurgling in his stomach, the cardinal was in no mood for antics.

The young priest fell in beside and half a pace back as Cardinal Messier ambled toward the exit and his waiting hover.

"What's your trouble, Father? You can't hide the look. You're an open book, and there's only one book I know better. Out with it, man."

Father Flores leaned close. "Father Ranier allowed two fugitives sanctuary late last night."

"Why's this the first I'm hearing of it?"

The simple answer was that the cardinal wasn't a young man any longer, and on the nights where he slept well, his staff didn't like to rouse him. Still, this was a mere political shindig. Ten of them a year in the parish, even in non-election years. Upstanding One Churchers didn't want to go into campaigning if they didn't have their own cardinal standing behind them. Someone could have pulled him away for a discreet word.

"Near as I've been able to gather, the police were hounding

Father Ranier with comms, so he shut off his datapad. He's been up all night waiting for someone to relieve him."

"It's a cathedral, not a Noodle-O-Rama. He could have sent word with any of the parishioners, got someone to round up a deacon to look after things. Well, I'll sort everything out when we get back."

Outside the hotel, the cardinal smiled and offered blessings in passing as a crowd greeted him. Father Flores raced ahead and opened the hover's door. The endless requests for favors and prayers obviated his need for haste.

When he reached the hover, the cardinal paused. Father Flores had more to say. If he ever made cardinal himself, Flores would need to develop a poker face before participating in the mayor's weekly card games.

"What else?"

Father Flores made a tentative gesture toward the rear seat of the hover. "Um. May I?"

There had to be more to this matter than wanting a more comfortable ride back to St. Ishmael's Basilica. Cardinal Messier allowed a sigh to escape his lips. "Very well."

So much for enjoying a moment's peace from his duties.

The door closed them in, and the hover rose. "These fugitives are in trouble with Civil Defense. One is believed to be a possible Earth spy; the other is Convocation."

"What?" Cardinal Messier bellowed.

He knew the tenuous position the Church faced these days. The Martian Circle was supposed to be a strictly defensive organization, a necessary counter to Earth's wizards in a time of war. However, their sinful methods grated on everything the cardinal believed.

Rubbing elbows with Richelieu was bad enough. But she was, as much as might be possible, a godly wizard. No credible accounts implied she was anything but an upstanding citizen and used the Lord's gifts with humility and restraint. She was, if anything, a drattedly inconvenient counterexample to the Church's narrative that the only good wizard was a non-practicing one.

In a way, he envied the woman, but that was his own sin to repent.

"It's hearsay, Cardinal. But it's from official channels. They haven't been inside St. Ishmael's. Father Ranier hasn't permitted them."

"Well," Cardinal Messier huffed. "At least we're being shown that much respect. I'll sort this all out. Father Ranier won't dare bar the door to *me*."

When the hover arrived out front, there was a police barricade and a crush of bodies blocking the stairs. The Basilica of St. Ishmael the Spacefarer rose above it all, its stone facade almost apologetic as if to say, "I tried to tell them, but they just won't leave."

Father Flores got out first and held the door again.

The police rushed up. A Civil Defense captain who had never been properly introduced barged into a conversation. "Your Eminence, one of your priests is sheltering two criminals."

Cardinal Messier walked past him.

"Well?" the captain pressed. "What are you going to do? Keep harboring a pair of enemies of Mars?"

Without turning back, the cardinal answered. "I'm going to enter my own cathedral."

When the door did not open at his approach, Cardinal Messier drew himself tall and knocked thrice. "This is Dustin Louis Michael Messier, Cardinal of New Singapore. I oversee this house of prayer in the name of our Lord. Open these doors at once."

Before he'd even finished, he could hear the ceremonial bar

being removed from the far side. The door swung open a cardinal's width a breath later. Though he was none too pleased that the portal wasn't thrown wide, Cardinal Messier stepped inside.

"Your Eminence! My prayers are answered!" Father Ranier greeted him, circling around to force the door closed with a shoulder as soon as the elder clergyman was inside. "They're respecting our sanctuary claim, but just barely. No one's being allowed in, and they're dragging off anyone who's left."

Cardinal Messier harrumphed. "We'll see about that. But first, where are these two supplicants you've taken in?"

Father Ranier glanced around the nave. Then he gave an apologetic smile and a shrug. "They're around here somewhere." The neophyte priest hustled off in search of them.

—————

Finding a deck of playing cards in a One Church cathedral had been something of a coup for Jessie Ramsey. While not exactly banned, cards were a gateway drug to gambling, and none of the starched collars would be caught dead with a pack. However, a degenerate attending a church-sponsored support group had been willing to part ways with one for a few of those new phony-baloney Martian marbits.

"Four on the five," Eric said, pointing in case Jessie couldn't connect the dots between the card in her hand and the one laid out in a traditional array on the bench of a pew.

While poker was a great way to blow off steam with friends or comrades, solitaire had long been an almost meditative exercise. With clear rules, easy decisions, and monotonous hand movements, it left the mind free to wander.

Provided, of course, someone's little brother would shut up and let her think. "Yeah. I see it."

"Just trying to help."

"Do you need me to scrounge up another deck?"

Eric craned his neck, looking up over the pew. "I don't think it's going to matter."

That answer didn't connect with her question. Jessie had known Eric long enough to pick up on the little disconnects between the various rails in his mental tram station. He was no longer operating within their previous conversation, and if she didn't want to lose track of him entirely, she was going to have to switch along with him.

One of the advantages of solitaire had been the excuse to keep her head down and use the relatively high-backed pews to shield her from view. Whatever else might be on her mind, the idea that Martian cops might storm the church at any moment never took a back seat. She was functioning on a half-hour nap and more cups of coffee than she cared to count.

When she followed her brother's worried look, she found two things.

First, and most obvious, was that weenie Father Ranier rushing toward the main doors.

Second, and she had to trust her brother's sixth sense that he saw it coming, was a booming knock at those doors.

Someone was here. And the priest had seen them coming.

Or someone tipped him off.

Geez, Jessie needed to clear her head. Shit like this should have been coming first and foremost to her head.

"I wonder who's here," Eric mused aloud.

"*This is Dustin Louis Michael Messier, Cardinal of New Singapore. I oversee this house of prayer in the name of our Lord. Open these doors at once.*"

"Thanks!"

The doors swung open with a suitably old-Earth creak.

"Your Eminence! My prayers are answered!" Father Ranier gushed.

"Finally," Jessie griped under her breath. "Now maybe we'll get a straight answer about some lodgings and a message to some lawyers."

Eric pulled her down. "Ix-nay. We need to find a back door."

"Why? This is their whole deal. Wanna help the downtrodden? We're the motherfucking downtrodden."

Eric clucked his tongue. "We're guests in this religion. Be nice." Then he remembered himself. "But also, we have to go because they're going to turn us over to the police and Convocation-lite, respectively."

"What makes you say that?" Jessie asked, straining to hear the hushed conversation that had followed the exuberance at the door. Given the acoustics in the place, she ought to have managed to snag at least a little of what the virtue ventriloquists were yakking about across the cathedral. At least, if Eric could shut his babble valve long enough to hear anything else.

"He's a wizard."

"Who's a wizard? Did they let one of your parole officers in?" Jessie asked, daring a quick peek.

"Cardinal Dustin Louis Michael Messier of the New Singapore diocese is a wizard. That's who. And the One Church only condones wizards for one task."

Jessie was at a loss but knew she had to take a guess or Eric would keep waiting. It was that damned didactic teaching he'd gotten in place of proper schools. "Talking to the dead?"

"No..."

"Something with changing wine into stuff?"

"No..."

"What?" Jessie snapped, careful to keep her voice low. She

didn't have time for these wizard riddles. Her guesses should have been plenty good enough to earn a direct answer by now.

"Sniffing out and suppressing other wizards."

"Oh. Oh, shit."

"Then again, Father Ranier did grant us sanctuary. It would look pretty bad if they reneged at this point."

"You're not going to have to wait long to find out," Jessie muttered.

Footsteps drew near. Soft. Tentative. Then they hastened and grew more confident. "Over here, Your Eminence!" Father Ranier glowered down at them from the end of the pew and lowered his voice. "Don't make me regret sheltering you. Be respectful and truthful with the cardinal. Sin can be forgiven, but only with repentance."

"Let me do the talking," Eric whispered.

Jessie fixed Eric with her best big sister frown. "That's my line."

At a concealed gesture from Father Ranier, the pair got to their feet. Jessie resisted an impulse to gather up the playing cards but decided to leave the innocuous game spread out on the pew as evidence of their harmlessness.

The cardinal was an elderly man, slack-skinned and slightly flabby, like someone had taken a hale and well-fed middle-aged man and slowly deflated him over the years. The outfit was One Church dating back to the Middle Ages of Earth. That lack of modern updates was a feature, not a bug, in church practices. He stared at each Ramsey in turn.

"You may remain until such time as you have repented your sins and negotiated a peaceful surrender to the proper authorities."

Jessie blinked in shock. Somehow, in the pit of her stomach, she'd expected to get handed over once someone able to read the political winds showed up on site. "Thank you, Your—"

"*YOU* will depart immediately," the cardinal continued, aiming a craggy finger at Eric. "You desecrate this house of God with every sinful breath you take."

"I'm not actually *with* the Convocation," Eric protested. "I haven't even used magic since we got here."

"The stench of it lingers on your soul. You use it even now. I will not stand for this evil in my presence. A penitent wizard deserves a chance to receive the grace of the Lord, but you are unrepentant. You pose a danger to the children under my protection, and I will not have it."

"Your Eminence, please," Jessie begged. "You can't throw him out there. They'll burn him alive!"

Frankly, Jessie didn't know what the martian wizards might do with a time traveler. Overly dramatic as it sounded, even as she suggested it, burning at the stake might have set the bar too low.

"God will not help those who turn away from him."

Jessie gritted her teeth. "Should have found a fucking synagogue." Her ancestors knew a thing or two about persecution that the One Church seemed to have forgotten.

"Look!" Eric called out. He'd snuck off while Jessie argued. When she and the cardinal turned to fix their attention on him, the wizard dunked a hand in a bowl of water held by a cherub statue. "See? Not evil."

Jessie raced over, pushing past the cardinal in the process. "Stop that! Get your hand out of there! That's their god's blood!"

Eric lifted a hand, dripping water. "No, it's not. It's holy water. And it should have burned me if I was—"

"OUT!" the cardinal bellowed. "Begone, wizard!"

Jessie took her brother by the shoulders and looked him in the eye. As usual, he glanced aside. "If you're doing any magic, stop it. This instant."

He mumbled something too soft to hear and too indistinct to lip-read.

"I'm serious. If you are, knock it off. Maybe they'll give us another chance."

"I'm never not doing magic. I can't help it."

"We're not ready to be out there. We have no plan. No backup. Just *try*."

"You stay. This is my mess."

"Like hell." Jessie grabbed her brother by the wrist, just like when they'd been kids and he'd wander off if left unattended. She marched toward the altar, veering right at the end of the pews. She called back without looking, "We're *both* leaving. And your VacationBlab rating's going in the shitter. At least do us the favor of not telling them we're coming."

The place had plenty of exits. By now, Martian Civil Defense must have had them all covered. But at least they weren't going to march out front and make things easy for them.

━━

James Rucker sat with his feet up on his desk, browsing reports on his datapad. He swiped through messages with the thumb of the hand holding the device, since his other hand was busy with a glass of wine that was receiving far more attention. Five-thousand-terra shoes scuffed the finish on real wood. Drops of red wine stained carpets that would cost most Martians a year's salary to rent for a weekend.

It was early for most people to be drinking, but James hadn't been to bed yet and considered this the end of his evening despite the presence of sunshine.

A knock at the door startled him. He sloshed his drink.

"Dammit! Fucking dammit, Sheena! I told you I was done for the night."

Sheena had been the one to knock. Her little rat-tat-tat couldn't be imitated. His assistant opened the door and peeked inside with a smile that was all apology. "Sorry, sir. But someone pulled rank on you."

"Shit. What is it?"

"We've got a Brenda."

James squeezed his eyes shut as if the pressure would wring some of the wine out of his brain. "Brenda... Brenda... which one's that? That an inbound smuggle?"

"Close, sir. Outbound."

"Outbound? Who wants *off* Mars these days? Half the fucking fleet's protecting us."

Taking the question as permission to enter, Sheena scurried across the office with a datapad held forth. James set down both his own datapad and the wine and took custody.

"Delete this," he said after absorbing the contents. "Then atomize the pad. We didn't have this conversation, and if anyone mentions Brenda, she was let go from accounting six months ago."

Sheena took the datapad back. "Understood, sir."

Once the door closed behind her, James opened a desk drawer. Fishing through a disorganized pile of devices, he found the one he was looking for. It was an older model datapad, scrubbed of all but a lone ID and the program to use it. He sent the comm request.

"*Yo. To what do I owe the pleasure?*"

"We got a top-down. Mixed double. Both under a dozen. Vacuum cases, but they got all the plugs. Eating some scrambled eggs and bacon. Let's get them an upgrade to the blue plate special."

"*Tags?*" came the reply. Korden hadn't missed a beat. He

knew James had been given orders from Esper to take custody of two fugitives—one male, one female, early twenties, spacers but with local connections—that were mixed up with the cops and needed transit to Earth. Or, frankly, anywhere but Mars.

"You clean and lonesome?" James pressed.

There was a brief pause. "*I am now.*"

"Jessie Ramsey and Eric Ramsey."

"*Fucking shit, boss. There's solar flares ain't as hot as them two.*"

"Did I ask your opinion?" James snapped. He waited, and there were no claims to the contrary. "You make this happen. Whatever else, those two kids are practically family."

"*How you want me to do this?*"

The unspoken version of the question was: "How do you *expect* me to do this?" James was asking the impossible, to pluck a pair of planetary-grade fugitives out of a live manhunt. It was only fair; Esper had asked the same of him. Korden was just the particular hill this shit was flowing down.

"We operate half the cargo coming and going from Mars." That was an exaggeration. The number wasn't even twenty percent, but for a core world, that still represented an incredible number of ships. "Dig into our reliable freelancers. Get a prio exit vector before they're off the grid. Zip before they catch up to the plan."

"*Got a plucker?*"

James pantomimed slamming his datapad on the edge of the desk several times. It was a voice comm, so Korden wouldn't see the gesture. But, seriously. Did he have to figure out every damn detail? Delegation was supposed to be a privilege of rank.

"I'll find someone. You get a light transport with a clean record and a pilot we can trust. And K-man... I want that shit lined up before I find that plucker."

As soon as he cut the comm, James began wracking his

brain. Who did he have in or near New Singapore who could facilitate that kind of close-up sleight of hand? Short list, that was for damn sure.

Still, the alternative was going back to Esper and trying to explain why the CDP had the Ramsey kids in custody.

Hell, if James Rucker had to fly out there and grab them himself, it would be less of a personal risk than pissing the boss lady off.

⌐⌐

"I'm coming. Let go of me," Eric insisted as Jessie reached for the push handle to the old-fashioned side door to St. Ishmael's. Figuring he wasn't going to run off at this point, she relented. He quickly shook the feeling back into his fingers and shot her a warning. "Wait."

She returned his glare, making sure he understood that this was the climb to the top of the roller coaster. Once she opened that door, they were committed to the ride. "We need to make a break for it."

"I can buy us a little time."

Could Eric not stay on the same file as her for one goddamn step of this plan? "You can work magic? I was sure they had this whole area on lockdown. Isn't that SOP?"

Eric didn't get into arcane details. "I can do enough to disguise us. They'll know something's up, but maybe it'll make them hesitate."

"Do it." Every muscle in her was tense, coiled, ready to spring. The waiting game wasn't her jam. They'd wasted time and allowed themselves to be surrounded. Now that their gambit had backfired, haste was key. She didn't trust those priests not to rat them out. Any second, the authorities could barge in, intercepting their escape before it fled the nest.

Eric balled his fist and crossed his forearms in an X. Then he briefly squeezed shut his eyes, and upon opening them, Jessie was gone. She caught a reflection of her new self in a pane of glass covering an old-fashioned notice board. In place of the woman she'd been was a teenage girl with blue eyes and red hair—Irish red, not the store-bought apple hue that was more literally red. He, in turn, was a brunette with dark eyes and a round face who was the dictionary definition of unremarkable. Both of them wore choir robes as if they'd been rehearsing when the police had surrounded the church.

Jessie took in their new personas in an instant. She rolled her eyes. "I guess it works." She cracked the door just wide enough to shout. "Two of us are coming out. Don't shoot!"

The Ramseys emerged from a side door, hands up. The "kindly don't shoot us" pose had been hammered into both as kids. Every game of space rangers, every loss in cops and smugglers, and many a surrender in hide-and-seek water blasters incorporated the motion.

From a cordoned-off barricade, police rushed them. Civil Defense officers kept blaster rifles trained in case of a trick, but Jessie spotted the fingers on trigger guards and aims slightly adjusted; they were more worried about mishaps than double crosses, which put modern Martian policing ahead of the corporate colonies and most of the borderlands.

As they were escorted by a black-clad wall of civic enforcement, a volunteer threw blankets over their shoulders like this was a wilderness rescue or a multi-day hostage crisis.

"We're fine," Jessie assured them. Her own voice sounded weird to her, so it must have been foreign to everyone else as well.

"Do you have hot cocoa?" Eric inquired. She only knew it was him by context. Not that he had the galaxy's deepest voice to begin with, but in that clarion teenage tone, he was unidentifiable. Of course, no one else would be angling for a sweet beverage, given the circumstances.

Then again, the sheer non sequitur of the request might have been great for selling their personas.

"It's them!" bellowed a deep, authoritarian voice. "Stop them!" It was Wizard Snow, and it had come from around the building. Eric's ploy hadn't gone unnoticed.

Reacting quickly, Jessie pointed a finger back toward the building. "I see them!" Then, she let out a shriek and grabbed Eric by the wrist.

They broke free of their police escort and plowed into the crowd. People jostled in equal measure to get out of their way and to press forward for a view of what was happening at the doors of the cathedral. This being a side entrance, the bystanders had by and large opted for more prominent exits to stake out. Jessie and Eric didn't have far to go to break into the clear.

Just as they got past the thickest part of the crush and into the casual passersby who were snooping on their way to more important errands, Jessie stumbled. Her gait shifted as her legs returned to her own.

Jessie also felt Eric's wrist grow larger and firmer within her grasp, and the bare skin became the fabric of a sleeve.

"THAT'S THEM!"

Jessie cursed wizards, busybody bystanders, and the year 2591. Rather than the cautious haste of a pair of choir singers trying to get out of the way of the action, they were back to the headlong rush of fleeing suspects.

The first vehicle that entered Jessie's line of sight was a hovercycle with a young delivery driver straddling the seat. He fixed a dumb animal stare on the Ramseys as Jessie made a beeline, drawing her blaster without breaking stride.

"Get off!" she ordered, gesturing with the weapon's barrel.

In that moment, she wouldn't have bet a marbit on the thing firing, but the delivery pilot didn't seem intent on trying. In his haste to remove himself from her way, the pilot tripped on his own cycle and spilled face-first onto the sidewalk.

Jessie swung a leg over the cycle and turned to find Eric right behind her. "Get on!"

Using her shoulder to balance, Eric climbed aboard behind her.

"Hold on!"

"Shouldn't we have helmeeeeeeeeeeeeeeeeeeeeeeeeeeets?" Eric shouted above the wind as Jessie gunned the engines and left an ion burn on the pavement.

For a delivery hovercycle, it had a real kick. Jessie had to double-check that her brother hadn't been thrown from the back, since he hadn't actually wrapped his arms around her as ordered.

But Eric wasn't the least bit concerned. He sat upright, even leaning to look down over the sides, admiring the view, as best she could discern.

Sirens wailed.

They had a head start, but there was never a question of the authorities not jumping in on the chase with both feet as soon as they got their heads out of their asses.

Jessie swerved and put buildings between the hovercycle and any potential lines of fire from the CDP. Between maneuvers, she accelerated. The speedometer climbed.

200 kph...

250...

300...

They blew past hovers traveling their same direction like they were oncoming traffic. Even ducking behind the windscreen, the wind threatened to tear Jessie's hair out by the roots.

Pressing against her back, Eric shouted into her ear to make himself heard over the hurricane howl of the wind. "Is this going to be a long chase? We have pepperoni, Hawaiian, and some kind of gourmet pizza with garlic pesto aioli."

Assuring they had a long enough straightaway in front of them, she spared her brother the most dire warning of their lives. "You'd better not be using *any* magic back there!"

At this speed, she couldn't imagine a scenario where they'd survive a loss of steering or attitude control.

Unfortunately, enclosed vehicles wouldn't have as much trouble with raw speed. Jessie either needed a change of vehicles or a change of tactics. New Singapore was a place two people could lose themselves in the haystack if they could break contact with pursuit long enough.

Jessie steered toward the city center.

The hovercycle tore through traffic, dodging slightly to avoid collisions. Jessie's heart pumped frantically to keep enough blood flowing to her muscles. Her brain fired neurons it only used in emergencies. One slip, and they'd be dead before they even felt it.

All the while, the sirens closed in.

More joined the chase, answering like wolves baying in the night. Jessie braked, slowing to non-racing speeds, and dumped the cycle on its side to use the main repulsors in a high-G turn. When they swerved around the PlanetBank's main headquarters on Mars, Jessie dove toward ground traffic.

"Do you know this area at all?" Jessie shouted over her shoulder. At this point, her lack of knowledge about New Singapore was a liability.

"I lived on the other side of the planet," Eric hollered back. "These big cities are all the same, confusing as a shopping mall."

Shopping mall? Now there was an idea.

Just then, a squad of patrol hovers rounded the PlanetBank building from the far side. They spotted the hovercycle and matched Jessie's hundred-story dive.

The ground rushed up to meet them, and a red rain of blaster fire fell around them.

"Fuckers!" Jessie couldn't believe they rated high enough for kill-on-sight live fire. A simple stun would kill them both and wouldn't dust civilians if the cops missed.

They couldn't keep this up. Jessie needed to find a place to disappear. To lose themselves in a crowd.

An advert board loomed over a pedestrian plaza, large enough to lay it down and play a game of football. It was playing a flatvid of a local newsfeed, and Jessie was framed in the center of the screen.

Eric noticed too—otherwise, he wouldn't have known which direction to wave to the camera.

Maybe this was his screwup.

Maybe he was a grown man and a wizard to boot.

But Eric was and always would be her little brother.

The worst Jessie faced was a Martian military prison, possible extradition to Earth, and execution as a deserter.

Jessie repeated her hard-turn maneuver, using the road below as additional reaction force to turn parallel to the ground. She had a new mission, and it wasn't about escaping. This was too high-profile. This was too big to slip away from and disappear into a crowd.

At least, it was too much to ask for both of them.

Where there were outdoor pedestrian malls in a city this size, there would be shopping centers nearby. Jessie spotted one and hunkered in her seat, trusting in the human ducking reaction to convince Eric to do likewise.

Shoppers screamed.

Jessie crashed through an automated door that didn't react

quickly enough for a hovercycle clocking over 100 kph. The cycle bucked at the impact, but Jessie maintained control, braking to adapt to the shortened sightlines and lack of civic engineering plans for indoor aerial traffic.

Inside, trapped and with limited options, shoppers ran in all directions. Jessie flared the engines and headed straight for a food court. She homed in on a sound that formed an instant plan in her mind.

"Be someone else!" Jessie ordered her brother as she reached back.

Families, gaggles of teenagers, and employees on meal breaks scattered as a hovercycle bulldozed tables out of its way.

Jessie swung the hovercycle past a large decorative fountain and used her own strength combined with the momentum of her turn to pitch Eric overboard.

He landed with a splash. She raced off in search of another exit to this place.

━━━

Eric stumbled to his feet, sopping wet and clinging to a half-eaten slice of pepperoni pizza. He had the presence of mind to alter his appearance while briefly submerged, rising from the water like one of the color-change plastic figures he'd had as a kid.

"Miss, are you all right?" someone asked.

Eric considered a voice before putting one on. "Uh, yah. I mean, that guy came completely from nowhere and, like, practically flattened me. My father is going to sue this place into next year."

A crowd gathered now. Jessie's stolen tech-bike had whined off into the distance. Everyone seemed to have come to the conclusion that it was safe now. They crowded around Eric, who now looked again like his choir-singer persona, albeit with an outfit he'd spotted on the rack at *Mi Armario* as Jessie sped them past.

"Did you get a look at them?" "Are you all right?" "Was that the terrorists from the newsfeeds?" "Do you have a lawyer?" "Lemme throw out that pizza for you." "Stay there; I'll find some napkins to dry you off." "Did you have a datapad? If this one's not yours, it's going to Lost & Found."

"Yeah, yeah, no, no, thanks, I'm set, no, it's all yours," Eric rattled off in teenage patois that was a good ten years out of date. But that's what the girls had sounded like *to him* every time he'd tried talking to them. The cadence changed from planet to planet, space station to space station; he'd picked the Martianest-sounding accent he could come up with on short notice.

It wasn't long before the police arrived. Or the Civil Defense Patrol. Eric was honestly having a hard time picking out the dividing line between the two. As a Convocation member, he hadn't had to deal with non-magical law enforcement, and the Martians had been happy to leave him to his own profession for oversight.

Uniformed patrol officers stormed in, blasters at the ready, armored like he and Jessie were going to potentially bomb them or something.

"Who saw what happened here?" one of the officers demanded, face obscured behind the half-visor of their helm, turning them into a black-headed egg with a mouth.

"She got knocked over by them," one of the nosy nearbys called out, pointing to Eric.

"Miss, were you able to ID the perps?"

"Oh. My. God! They were perps?" Eric whirled on the crowd. "Why did no one, like, mention that? Ew! One of them touched me."

"What did they look like?" the officer pressed as his comrades fanned out to search the area on foot. He held up a datapad with front and side views of Jessie and someone's sketched versions of the same poses for Eric.

Eric studied the flatpics briefly, then gave a melodramatic shrug. "Ugh. Like blurs? These people are clearly *not* blurry, and the ones who played billiards with me—knocked me over without a single care about my new outfit—clearly *weren't* clear at all. Like, maybe instead of standing there playing picture book quiz with me, maybe you should, like, chase that bicycle."

"Bicycle?" the officer echoed in puzzlement.

Crap. He should have danced around the technical term for the type of vehicle. But that's what it was... a flying bicycle with science instead of pedals. He had to play this off as the officer's problem. "Gah. Be old somewhere else."

Just then, a girl about Eric's apparent age rushed up with two hands full of absorbent napkins with the Redburgers logo printed on them—a stylized hamburger with devil horns. Eric and the girl parted around, daubing away inconsequential amounts of the fountain water soaking him.

As the police moved on, the crowd lost interest. Eric gently brushed away his helper's soggy wad of napkins. "Thanks. But if you could help a girl out, I need some fresh out's." He hoped the slang term for outfits hadn't shifted in the past five years. Or ten. He hadn't exactly been on the cutting edge during college, either. "Can you pick me out something cute—I'm trusting your fashion sense, babe—and bring it to the washroom for me?" Luckily, the weird new Martian coins Eric had been collecting the past few hours had come along for the ride when he'd altered his form. He dug out what he hoped was a sizable sum for a single change of clothes.

His helper leaned close. "What size?"

Well, this one would be embarrassing to get wrong. Eric

shut his eyes briefly, then rattled off a list that could get fed straight into one of those knitting machines popular out in the colonies. "Slim, small, 32A, 73—but go short sleeves—58, knee length, small, full-calf, and 6 flats."

The girl stared at the pile of coins in her hands. "You... want everything?"

"You need more?" Eric asked, now fearing that he'd underpaid her.

The girl shook her head vigorously.

Eric marched off to the washroom as his would-be rescuer rushed over to *Mi Armario*.

Now that he considered it, the girl was close to his size. And even if it didn't work out that she could just keep the clothes and wear them, maybe *Mi Armario* would let her exchange them for the right size.

When Eric walked back out of the washroom a moment later, all that was left of his choir singer persona was a puddle in one of the stalls. No one batted an eye as a strange man exited. The washrooms were busy enough, and Mars wasn't some backward colony that segregated washrooms by gender.

He crossed paths with his helper, who bore an armload of shopping bags, acquired with admirable haste. The quick smile he spared her went ignored, which was as good a sign as any that his disguise had worked. He appeared closer to forty now than his usual twenty-two—or the twenty-seven he should have been. A square jaw, wisps of gray at his temples, and a strut of totally unearned confidence helped him blend in seamlessly with a whole different classification of shopper.

Now...

Where the hell had Jessie gotten off to?

Jessie ducked again as the hovercycle crashed through the decorative bushes surrounding the balcony-level outdoor dining area of this mall's Marko Parko. The whole ordeal up until now had been stressful. From keeping her brother from toppling a hundred stories to his death to avoiding mass murder by losing control of a high-speed vehicle indoors and everything in between, her focus had been pulled in multiple urgent directions at once.

Now, she was free.

Blaster fire ripped past her.

Sort of free, she amended mentally.

Now, it was just her and the Martian authorities. Her assets were her skills, her wits, a stolen blaster that may or may not have recovered from turning into an accessory for a teenage One Church girl, and an equally stolen delivery hovercycle with obvious shortcomings as far as getting offworld.

But she only had to worry about herself.

Eric was on his own now. Splitting up had been necessary to give him a shot to shake pursuit. That plan relied on Jessie occupying everyone's attention to the point where Eric Ramsey, bumbling wizard-school dropout, became an afterthought.

She sponsored the mission herself. She accepted. She was up to the task and would give the mission every drop of blood in her body if that was what it took.

Plan A: Put distance between herself and security forces closing in on all sides. Go to ground. Lay low. Search for her brother and get off Mars together.

More blaster fire sizzled past, and Jessie was forced to angle back toward the surface, where civilians would give the supposed "good guys" pause before they continued firing her way. Still, it made Plan A sound pie-in-the-sky. Far from losing her pursuit, she was gaining pursuers steadily as she evaded the current idiots.

Plan B: Turn the tables. Set an ambush for one of those patrol hovers. Take hostages. Negotiate.

Sounded like a blaze-of-glory plan. If Jessie hadn't been lettering the plans in order of conception, she'd have bumped that one down to the back of the alphabet.

Plan C: Find Esper. Play on family ties and beg for protection. Open a full broadside of battleship plasma cannons into her political career.

As much as it might work, Jessie couldn't bring herself to do it. Maybe if she still had Eric with her. But she had to believe he could Ramsey his way out of this with enough of a distraction drawing eyes off him. Jessie couldn't destroy Esper's life just to save her own.

She banked the hovercycle as more patrol hovers approached from ahead. Was it her imagination, or were they trying to herd her more than catch up to her?

The moment she realized it, Jessie found the ambush. An upward rain of red plasma shot into the sky. With aerial traffic diverted out of the area, ground forces were green-lit to fire with a backdrop of empty sky.

Jessie cringed and waggled the hovercycle as she attempted to regain lost altitude.

Plan D: Ram through a skyscraper window and deal with whoever might be inside.

Plan E: Race blaster fire to the nearest starport, Discovery Memorial, and find a ship to hijack.

Plan F: Controlled crash and dive clear of wreck site. Roll to absorb lethal momentum.

Plan F had been inspired by one of the blaster bolts catching one of the two main repulsors on the hovercycle. Barring a miracle of the sort Jessie wasn't raised to expect, she wasn't going to get another kilometer before gravity took her into custody.

Followed closely by the crazy new Martian authorities in this civil war timeline.

As the ground rose up, Jessie timed one last skid turn, realizing she'd been sheepdogged practically back to where she'd dumped Eric. At one end of the pedestrian plaza, there was a pocket of walkable green space—little more than a couple walking paths and some lawn. The hovercycle fought to resist its own forward momentum, lone repulsor flaring. With a final kick of the ion engine, Jessie leapt free as the hovercycle zoomed off to slam into a parked sedan.

Grassy turf and open sky swirled around her as Jessie rolled, battered, and buffeted until she slid to a stop, fighting for breath.

"Freeze! Stay down!"

Barely able to move, Jessie put up her hands as she lay on her back. A stampede of uniformed justice trampled her, rolling her facedown, pinning her arms behind her and mag-cuffing them there.

As she was dragged to her feet to the cheers of onlookers, Jessie came up with a new plan.

Plan G: Hold out under interrogation as long as possible so Eric has time to get away.

They'd break her sooner or later.

Hours later, Jessie sat in a drab duracrete room with faded green tint on the walls and glossy black surveillance hemispheres watching from the ceiling. Her chair was all steel, bolted to the floor at the center of the room. Her ankles were secured to the chair's legs with wide straps, made of hyrdro-stabilized polymer weave—if prisoner technology hadn't advanced in the past few years. The chair had no arms, leaving Jessie's straight at her sides, wrists held firm by more of the same straps. One final cinch around her chest kept Jessie from slouching or squirming.

They'd stripped her, searched her, scanned her, hosed her down, treated the injuries she'd sustained in the crash, and dressed her in an orange jumpsuit. Beneath the garment, a wrap around her ribcage leaked bio-regenerative gel that was speeding the knitting of her cracked ribs. Nice of them. Nicer would have been *also* not tightening a restraint around broken bones.

No chrono marked the time. She was hungry but didn't feel like eating, thirsty but unwilling to trust anything the Martians might bring her to drink. Psychotropic agents in the water were a time-honored classic to soften up a prisoner about to be interrogated.

Jessie tried to remain still. Every squirm came with the click of a ratchet as the straps auto-tightened to fight any attempt at getting loose. Her bare feet grew chilled from the floor.

The door opened. Jessie was faced away from it. She didn't dare attempt to twist to see behind her.

"Good afternoon, Lieutenant." The voice was pleasant enough. Perversely, that was a bad sign. The nutjobs always made it sound like they enjoyed their work.

"Jessica Judith Ramsey, Lieutenant First Class, Earth Navy. Serial number—"

"Enough of that. We have your whole file on record. Most of what was formerly Earth Navy fights for Mars now. But you wouldn't know that, would you?"

Jessie held her tongue. This was a marathon, not a debate. There were no bonus points for right answers, no moral victories for proving him wrong. So long as she had teeth and fingernails, this asshole was getting nothing.

Then, the asshole stepped into view. He wore a familiar-style uniform. It was Earth Navy in all but insignia. A commander by the oak leaf. Chowaniec by the nameplate. She knew many of the ribbons by sight, but the newer ones were all gibberish.

"Five years is a long time to be gone. I was Earth Navy five years ago, same as you. If not for your brother's misbegotten magic, I suspect you'd be Martian Navy too, these days."

"All a big misunderstanding," Jessie agreed. "Untie me and hand me a blaster. I'm in."

"Cute. But no. Unfortunately, the things that *did* happen, *have* happened. We can't pretend they didn't. For instance, your brother..." Chowaniec stepped out of view and tapped at a datapad. "How'd they put it? Ah, yes. He 'ripped the fabric of time and space, at the peril of all existence.' Wizards. Even the ones who joined the Martian Circle are stuffy old coots. Mostly former Earth Navy liaisons. If you served with any, there's a good chance they're with us now."

"What's this? A history lesson?"

"You could use one, couldn't you?" Chowaniec countered. He paced circles around Jessie, daring her to try to track him. "Frankly, I don't think we can have a particularly productive conversation until you understand this new galaxy you find yourself in. We didn't start this war. Earth forced our hand when they let the Convocation run amok."

"What did happen?" Jessie asked, curiosity getting the better of her plan to completely stonewall this schmuck.

"Six seats. Six wizard senators. No more. No fewer. It was right there in the ARGO charter. But the wording was tricky. It said Convocation. They ran unaffiliated wizards for normal seats. I can't say what irregularities might have taken place, because *we* were never allowed to investigate. But when the coalition government formed, we ended up with our first wizard prime minister. And the rules started going right down the waste reclaim."

Jessie swallowed hard, her dry mouth making things difficult.

She'd had her share of interactions with wizards. Mostly, they were harmless, from cranky charlatans like Uncle Enzio to dreamy cloud-watchers such as Eric to do-gooders like Aunt Esper. The star-drive mechanics she'd met in the navy had been all right. More senior wizards assigned to ships' security tended to be gruff, arrogant, and strictly business.

Politically ambitious wouldn't have been how she would have described any of them.

Well, up until she'd seen Esper campaigning for President of Mars.

"So, boo hoo, you got bossed around by wizards."

"Wizards conquered Earth," Chowaniec countered. "Those six seats they had was the compromise between making sure their interests were looked after and ensuring they didn't ever run the show."

"I'm not political. Sorry. Poli-sci majors can't shoot straight and fly like taxi pilots. So, if you want to skip to the part where you beat the shit out of me, let's get on with our day."

To her surprise, Chowaniec chuckled. "You will not be harmed in our custody."

"So long as I talk." It was a tired old game. Cat. Mouse. Set expectations. Subvert them. Offer hope. Dash it. If he had access to her files, Chowaniec had to know she'd gone through counterintelligence training.

"On the contrary." He swiped a few times and held up a datapad in front of her to read. "You'll be treated strictly in accordance with the Martian Alliance of Represented Systems Charter and the Mars Navy Code of Justice."

She squinted to read the fine print, but he didn't seem interested in letting her scan the whole document or even get a good look at the page on screen.

"Long story short, your treatment will follow these rules verbatim. Interrogations are limited to eight hours per session. That leaves you five hours strapped to that chair in exact accordance with paragraph seven of prisoner treatment. Per the rules, you are allowed a minimum of two hours in your cell between interrogations. You will be allowed four hours sleep per night. You will be given the exact nutritional content required over the span of your mandated two meals, which we will force-feed you if you refuse to eat, along with a painstakingly measured ration of water. You will have access to a toilet in your cell and are entitled to one shower per week."

"What if I need to take a shit right now?" Jessie demanded. If they wanted to find a way to *really* torture her, a diabolically strict adherence to rules and schedules would do it. Special forces came with flexibility. She'd *earned* herself latitude.

"Go right ahead. Four hours and fifty-two minutes from now, you'll be escorted to your cell, where you can rinse out the stains in the toilet. A fresh jumpsuit will be issued after your shower next Thursday between your morning and afternoon interrogation sessions."

"Until you break me," Jessie reasoned.

Chowaniec cracked a smile. He crouched in front of her. "To what end? To divulge classified information that a thousand other officers in Mars Navy already had access to? To glean five-year-old secrets we already knew, from a time when our enemies fought on our side?"

"Why, then? I'll never help you find my brother."

"Not intentionally. But according to reports from the

Martian Circle, he's a bit of an idiot as wizards go. He's liable to try to save you. You're bait."

"Then why the interrogations?"

Her interrogator's smile fell. "Because when you arrived here on Mars, in the present, you treated Mars as the enemy. If you had turned yourself in, after a debrief and getting you back up to speed, you'd have been a valuable asset. Instead, you turned Mars into your own private war zone. People got hurt out there. Good people. *My* people. Fellow Martians." He slapped the back of a hand against the datapad. "And here it tells me what I can and can't do to you while I've got you here."

"And it doesn't say anything about a trial or extradition or— or..." She was running out of legalese. Ramsey upbringing had been scant on the getting out of trouble part of the law.

The smirk Chowaniec gave her was downright devilish. "You know, there's some ongoing debate over that. After all, since we're going *so* by the book... legally, you've been declared dead."

―――

Life had returned to normal in the plaza with appalling ease. A civil defense cordon became a salvage area became a cleanup site became a gardening reclamation became a tiny little park again. All over the course of a couple hours.

Not knowing what else to do, Eric wandered the plaza on foot, bereft.

It was all so... normal.

No more frantic chasing. No more suspicious priests. No police. No sign of Mars Circle—or was it Martian Circle? He could only guess by the sigil what they might call themselves.

Peace all around.

None inside.

They'd taken Jessie. He'd brought her here. Showing off, he'd lost control. Secrets were a sibling thing. All he wanted was to show her that he wasn't a loser for getting thrown out of Oxford. Now, he'd made her a deserter, an accomplice, a prisoner.

It was all his fault.

Eric sniffled, rubbing an eye with the back of a fist.

"Are you lost, little boy?"

It took a second for Eric to realize the woman's voice was directed at him. He'd shifted personas twice more since the washroom, not wishing anyone to find his lingering suspicious. Currently, he wore the shape of an eight-year-old boy.

Eric shook his head.

"Where are your parents?" The woman interrogating him was old enough to have a son about his apparent age. Conservative dress. Jewelry. Cosmetics. Well-off, but in a standard core world way.

"Don't know,' Eric answered truthfully. He had ideas, but venturing any of them aloud wasn't going to help anyone, least of all him.

Lost in his own troubles, Eric didn't know quite what was happening until he found himself at a table at the outdoor food court, sitting under an umbrella with a family of four, poking at a cup of pistachio ice cream with a plastic spoon.

It was good ice cream.

A brother and sister, maybe ten and twelve respectively, tried to engage him in conversation, to cheer him up. But all Eric could see were younger versions of himself and Jessie. Rather than reply, he stuffed more of the ice cream into his mouth.

What could he say to them?

Nothing but lies would do.

He wasn't really a kid. He was a grown man—sort of. Jessie

never treated him like an adult. But why should she? A wizard? What kind of wizard was he?

Actually, that was an excellent question.

Jessie had been taken prisoner, and he hadn't even come up with a plan to break her out of jail. He was a Ramsey, after all. Jessie might not know quite what that meant, but Eric had heard all Enzio's old stories. Mom wasn't the rebel; she was the reasonable one. Dad wasn't a washed-up nobody; he was a master criminal who wanted his kids to have better role models than him. Uncle Roddy planned heists. Aunt Yomin hacked syndicate computers.

And Uncle Enzio was Mordecai The Brown.

As the father of the family who'd taken custody of him yakked on his datapad, Eric's mind wandered.

He needed a plan.

Plan A for a wizard was always violence.

Right and wrong were relative. Hurting people was wrong. Letting family get hurt was wronger. How many people might he have to murder to achieve Jessie's release? Was there a number he could balance on his own personal scales? Uncle Enzio always claimed there was no number of strangers who could balance the scales against a single person you cared about.

But Eric could hardly imagine being so callous. He might have learned magic from Enzio, but he had his own ideas about morality.

OK, so Plan A was out.

Plan B: Rewind time so none of this ever happened. No arrest. No Earth/Mars War. No Martian Circle—or Mars Circle. Esper wouldn't have to run for president. Aunt Michelle's restaurant wouldn't fail. Eric would think better of trying to jump a second into the future and just enjoy a nice meal with Jessie.

That whole notion was a warm fuzzy dream wrapped in impenetrable, spiky, poisoned, red-hot steel. He'd do it in the snap of his fingers if snapping could pull it off. As it stood, his theoretical reverse time-travel spell wasn't even a complete idea.

All right, then. Plan B was going to take longer than was currently feasible.

Plan C was finding his way to Uncle Enzio. It would likely result in Plan A all over again, but with the added benefit of fewer nightmares. Of course, Jessie would be subject to Hades-only-knew what in some stinking police dungeon. She might even get shot as a deserter. Or a spy. Whichever they decided she was.

Plan D involved a rousing speech on the holovid that ended the war with Mars and resulted in Jessie no longer being caught between opposing sides.

Plan E involved sneaking invisibly into a secure military facility that undoubtedly had wizards factored into their security and sneaking back out with Jessie invisible too.

Plan F was to hire mercenaries to storm the prison.

Plan G was to comm Dad for advice.

Plan H had Eric turning everyone he came across into a doppelganger of Jessie, from people on the street to the guards at the prison, until no one could tell which Jessie was real and they escaped in the chaos.

Plan I got skipped because an "I" looked too much like a one.

Plan J was to join Earth's war efforts and help defeat Mars, freeing Jessie as part of a general amnesty.

"Ollie, these nice men are going to help you find your parents."

Eric blinked. Ollie? Right. That was the name he'd given

the family. He reoriented himself to his surroundings. Two police officers—regular old New Singapore Police Department, not the paramilitary civil defense soldiers—loomed over him, trying their hardest not to look scary and failing badly.

One held out a hand. "Come on, kiddo. We'll get you home in time for dinner."

"Or at least dessert," the other added.

Plan K...

Eric reached out a hand and allowed himself to be towed away from the family who'd temporarily adopted him.

Jessie was probably in a police station somewhere. These two were going to take him to a police station. Seemed as good a place as any to start.

He reached back to wave and pocketed a clean napkin, tucking it away for later as Plan K started coming together.

Jessie stumbled and caught her balance on the far side of the cell door after the shove from the guard. Stiff joints ached at the sudden, jerky motion after being held immobile for so long.

White on white on white. No contrast anywhere in the cell. Two meters and change on a side, nearly half the space was taken up by a slab bunk jutting from the far wall. If that mattress was a millimeter over the absolute minimum allowed by prisoner treatment laws, she'd have been shocked.

"See you in four hours," Chowaniec told her.

"What about my two hours of downtime?" Jessie demanded.

"Four's more than two. Get some sleep. Or don't. I honestly don't care."

That much Jessie believed.

Her cell door slid shut, locking into place flush with the

surrounding wall, discernible only as a faint seam between panels.

Jessie rubbed her wrists, raw from both the straps for the past eight hours and the too-tight mag cuffs on her way to her cell. Then, after a cough, she wiped her nose.

Damn them.

Sure, they'd brought her a tray of food. Told her to eat. But they'd also left her secured to the chair, unable to do so. Taking that as official refusal of food, they'd forced a tube down her throat and pumped nutrient gel into her stomach. There was no reason to expect future meals to go any differently.

Jessie's sole task became plotting an escape. Prisoner-of-war training had largely focused on prominent xeno factions and common pirate practices. She had preset plans to adapt for breaking out of an eyndar POW camp, a plouph prison labor colony, or zheen slave breeding site. But in an almost embarrassing failure of self-awareness, looking in retrospect, she hadn't been coached on breaking out of ARGO military jails.

First time for everything.

Because what Chowaniec had said about being bait rang a little too true. Eric might not have been classical hero material, but he had a blithe confidence and disconnection from reality, probability, statistics, and the horrors of what failing with life-and-death stakes might look like.

Time was everything.

Not only would the regimen of forced immobilization and malnourishment wear her down and decrease her capabilities, but the longer this went on, the more time Eric had to try something stupid. He was a worrier with a vivid imagination. Bad as things might get for Jessie, they'd pale compared to what her brother might convince himself she was going through.

Worse yet, he was doomed to fail. Eric had already

demonstrated a lack of understanding of his own limits. Otherwise, they wouldn't have gotten stranded outside their own time.

Priority one was finding a guard she could overpower. Prisons didn't assign guards who made great punching bags. The marine corporal who'd manhandled her down the hall was pumped full of pharma and armored but not armed. There would be no weapon to confiscate. Assuming he was typical of what she could expect, any confrontation would start off with her at a fifty-kilo disadvantage with no protection and without a good meal in her for days now.

Still, she'd been trained to fight to win. If she was willing to risk cracking a trachea or driving nasal cartilage into a guy's brain, she had a shot. Chowaniec was nothing to worry about. He might be in military shape, but only desk-job shape. If that guy had seen combat in the past two decades, she'd eat her jumpsuit.

After that...

Well, she had more planning to do. These assholes weren't likely to share a map of the facility with her, so she'd be on her own. Best case, she'd ambush someone and acquire a weapon before the general alarm went up. A valuable enough hostage, and she might see sky over Mars.

No more fucking around if she got that far. The Red Planet would be in her rear scanners the instant she found Eric.

Jessie let out a breath and sat on the cot. She could feel the slab straight through the mattress. It was her only companion in the cell.

Only.

Companion.

Geez. This cell didn't even have a toilet. On the floor between her feet, a small grate offered its services.

Shoulders stiff, Jessie began the struggle to work her way

out of her jumpsuit before making use of the limited facilities Mars Navy had provided.

It wasn't a great omen for the rest of her plans.

James Rucker got the comm as he was flying over to meet with one of his quietest operators. Jessie Ramsey was in custody.

There would be consequences for that. But how was *he* supposed to slide those two dumbasses off the grid if they ran around topside practically blaring their presence?

Bad enough Cardinal Messier hadn't played ball.

Bad enough the cops couldn't corral both of them.

Bad enough Eric Ramsey was still wandering around on the loose.

At least James could keep track of the one that Mars Navy had. Finding a wizard before his own people rounded up Eric Ramsey was going to be a planetary-grade pain in the ass.

Set to silent, James's datapad buzzed in his pocket. Fuck. Even in private mode, there was a select number of individuals who could get a hold of him no matter what.

"Hey, babe," he answered, identifying the caller as he lifted the device to his ear.

"*Little Earl's got his debate tonight,*" Sharee reminded him. Dammit. That was one of the problems sending a kid to an expensive private school; Earl had gotten involved with a debate team. James had grown up where a blaster settled most arguments, not judges. If his son wasn't careful, he'd end up a lawyer or politician.

"Yeah. Just gotta take care of some stuff."

"*This better not be stuff. I'm not covering for you. You can tell him yourself if you don't show up.*"

"Yeah, babe. I know. I might be late, but I'll be there." He cut the comm before this conversation dragged out.

Sharee he could placate later. Esper would be a harder sell if her godkids got themselves stapled to a fence post.

When he arrived at a closed landing yard outside a construction site, James got out, leaving the door to his hover open. If he needed a quick exit, that would be one fewer step in the process.

"You're late."

James whirled. Jesus. But it was just McCullough. He was dressed in civilian clothes, but it was hard to see him as anything but Mars Navy.

"You're lucky I don't pack these days. Sneakin' up on a guy..."

"I think I already know why you commed." McCullough was no-nonsense. Part of why he kept getting business.

There was no point sparring or dumping any incriminating information that wasn't strictly necessary. "What've you got for me, then?"

"It's a stone chicken. Never getting off the ground."

"Not a great answer. I better not be missing my kid's thing for a dumb barnyard analogy."

"We're expecting a prisoner exchange with the blue guys."

James barked a single laugh in derision. "You want me to deal with the Earthlings for her?"

McCullough shrugged, hand tucked in his jacket pockets. "Best I can do is an itinerary for the transfer."

"A list of the guards with direct contact."

A buzz-cut-topped head was already shaking before James finished his demand. "Can't do that."

"Five names. I can work with that."

"A line I can't cross."

James fixed the naval officer with a glare that threatened

murder. "You ever think what happens if I have to go over your head? You ain't the last option on my list."

McCullough scoffed. "Maybe back in your uncle's day. You people don't have the muscle to throw around anymore. I expect full compensation once I transmit the flight plan."

"Forget it."

McCullough cocked his head. "I don't think you're considering the consequences."

"Consequences? I export that shit, asshole. You're off the payroll."

McCullough took a step toward him, but James Rucker didn't scare easily. "You're making a mistake."

"You're gonna bounce. And my next comm will get this cleaned up. If I catch your shadow coming up behind me, I'll be hiring for a twofer on the cleanups, *capisce*?"

McCullough scowled as he backed away, that navy-issued brain of his grinding gears on how to delegate this problem when he was operating outside the chain of command. He might have been a good source in the past, but James was willing to burn this bridge rather than let an informant think coughing up info was optional.

He hadn't made it all the way back to his hover when his datapad signaled another incoming comm.

"You better have better news," James warned Korden without any greeting in either direction.

"Old hand lined up. Officially on the ground waiting for a rush delivery. Exit clearance a finger snap away."

Finally. At least something was going right. "Right. Sit on him. Pay what it costs."

"On it, boss."

James disconnected the comm, then ducked into his hover and sat there.

Slowly, he scrolled through his contacts. Idly, he hoped that a name would jump out at him as an alternative.

Whatever else he might be, James was Martian to the core. Mars Navy might be poking a hornet's nest right now, but they were the good guys. And this comm was going to cost a lot of good men and women their lives.

He had the evacuation lined up. The hard part was going to be the extraction.

The depths of James's comm ID list were filled with people who'd been granted amnesty for past crimes, some of whom shouldn't have been. Cold-blooded killers and hothead leg-breakers, con men and protection money collectors, drug kingpins and pimps, safecrackers and computer hackers.

None of the others had the skills needed to pull off a job like this.

James gritted his teeth as he tapped the name.

The comm connected in short order. *"You finally get tired of fucking this dog. I'll walk it right out of there."* The voice was middle-aged, female, and dripping disdain. But at least she was keeping abreast of the newsfeeds.

"How close are you?"

"Close enough. Get me clearance to land; I'll take it from there."

"I've got an exit lined up for two."

"Eric's a big boy. He can look out for himself. And I'll handle the extraction."

"She wants them both taken care of."

"I don't work for her. He's your problem."

The mention of work brought up a sticky issue. Not that James was ever short on funds, but beyond a certain sum, it was hard to make this sort of expense disappear into the logistics department operating budget. Fifty or a hundred thousand marbits for consulting fees was steep but workable for a good accountant. Some auditor starts seeing eight- and nine-figure payments, questions come hard and fast.

"How much this going to cost me?"

"*Your lucky day. She's on my list. This one's gratis.*"

"Thanks."

"*It's not a favor for you, you shit-brained middleman. Just keep your fuckwit goons out of my way.*"

The comm cut off abruptly.

James let out a long sigh and ran the fingers of both hands through his hair. It was over. Done with. Oh, he'd check in later just as a matter of due diligence. But Jessie Ramsey was as good as off Mars already. Once Eric turned up, he'd get the kid into a hover and reunite the pair offworld somewhere.

Discarded on the seat beside him, the datapad showed the time.

James had time to get to Little Earl's debate. In fact, he'd hardly be late.

———

People bustled in and out. Voices everywhere. No one was happy to be here. Too many smells to discern them individually, though human sweat was definitely among them. All manner of dress, with the exception of anything that could be considered "nice." People had been dragged in wearing pajamas, shirtless, dressed for street work, sporting fresh rips and tears, patched with red-soaked cloth pads showing off amateur scientific healing. Others wore uniforms, drab, stern, and unwelcoming.

Eric sat at a desk behind the low wall that separated the waiting and datawork areas. Still in his Ollie disguise, his feet dangled just above the floor, the plastic chair being sized for adults.

After a few questions and a scan of his thumb, the officers had left him alone with instructions not to wander off.

Someone had also kindly provided some mistreated Wax-i-Rods, presumably to occupy him with an aim toward him following that one mandate.

Officer Grissom returned and sat down on the main side of the desk, across from Eric. He was balding, with a weathered face that tried to smile but looked like the effort hurt. He clasped his hands, a telltale sign he was about to deliver bad news.

"I've got some bad news."

Eric looked up from his napkin and set down his red Wax-i-Rod, giving the police officer his full attention.

"We ran that thumb scan, but it looks like there was a data error. Colonial stuff. Nothing to worry about right now. But it means we haven't ID'ed your parents yet."

Eric would very much have liked to know what his thumb scan had turned up. Just not enough to speak to the police. He was in enough trouble already without saying things. Between Mom and Dad's lessons and his shift into the Convocation track for justice, he'd never been in custody before. This wasn't a great time to be pedaling with stabilizers.

"Don't worry. We've got a comm in to Child Services. They'll have a social worker here soon to get you a place to sleep tonight."

Eric offered a tight-lipped smile in thanks, a signal that he understood standard English.

With the relevant information exchanged, Eric returned his attention to Plan K.

"What're you drawing there?" Grissom asked. Angling his head as if he could read any better that way. And it *was* reading he'd be trying for if he puzzled out what Eric was working on, not deciphering some childish doodle.

Without looking up, Eric continued his work a moment longer. He was almost done...

"Some kind of story?"

With a slight flourish, Eric finished the final lines. Then navigating a clutter of takeout boxes and police gizmos, he slid the napkin across the wide desk, twisting it to face Officer Grissom along the way.

A smirk and a chuckle accompanied the note's arrival. At first, it was clear that the words hadn't registered. "What font is this?"

"It's calligraphy," Eric replied, the first words out of his mouth since meeting the officers at the plaza.

Officer Grissom squinted, clearly struggling.

Block letters. Simple. Like on datapads.

It was a shame to waste his best Wax-i-Rod calligraphy, but this scientist was barely literate, it seemed. The writing squirmed into less ornate text.

The look of horror that grew on Officer Grissom's face had less to do with fluid wax on a napkin and more with the words it formed.

There is no one from the Mars Circle here to protect you. You have taken my sister hostage. Release her quietly and do not attempt to follow us. You are MY hostage.
Eric Ramsey, Order of Chronos

"Is this a joke?" Officer Grissom demanded, slapping the back of his hand against the napkin like it was a suspect who wouldn't talk.

"Was it funny?" Eric asked.

"No, it's not fucking funny, kid."

"Then it wasn't a joke. Go get my sister." The look of terror in those eyes that wouldn't meet Eric's told him that his message was getting through. Scaring people was mean, but it was better than actually hurting them.

"I don't even know *who* has your sister. Sure as hell isn't us."

A hard hand thudded down on Eric's left shoulder. "Eric, that's not nice."

Another hand came down on his other shoulder. "Whatever little trick you just worked was the last little clue. We've been sniffing around for hours, never quite able to pick you out of the crowd."

"You his parents?" Grissom asked, clearly baffled at the turn of events.

"His parole officers," Snow replied. "This one's our problem." He reached out a fist and pressed a ringed finger to Eric's napkin, leaving a scorched sigil of the Mars Circle behind.

"Uh. OK. Yeah. I'll just need you to—"

Slater interposed herself between the officer and Eric. "You do whatever your department guidelines require. We're taking our Class A prisoner directly to a secure facility."

"Oh. Sure. Right."

The two wizards marched Eric out of the police station as all eyes in the building followed them.

Outside, Snow harrumphed. "Have a little self-respect. Take your true form."

With a sigh, he felt their wills relax just enough to allow Eric to look like Eric again instead of Ollie.

A black hover with dark-tinted windows pulled up. The pilot got out and opened a door for them.

"I'll make you a deal."

Slater and Snow got a chuckle out of that. "You're not in much of a position to bargain."

"I just want my sister freed."

"Oh, is that all?" Slater asked sarcastically as the pair ushered him toward the hover.

He allowed himself to be sandwiched into the back seat between them. The hover rose as soon as the pilot was back at the controls.

"I promise, if you get her released from whoever has her, I'll come along quietly."

Snow shook his head. "We don't get involved in scientific matters."

Eric leaned forward to see past Slater and out the window as Martian cityscape rushed past them. "Well, would it change your policy if I said the alternative was I killed all the tech in this hover and nullified the gravity stone when we hit the ground?"

"You wouldn't," Snow countered.

"You couldn't," Slater added.

"I will. I can. And if you think a quick death is my biggest fear, I think you're underestimating how much I love my sister."

"Land."

"Yes, sir." The hover angled slightly downward.

"NOW!"

The angle of descent steepened into a full-on dive.

"Agree, or we all die," Eric assured them. Martian buildings had a new, external lift rocketing toward the ground floor. He didn't have long to finish this negotiation. Eric concentrated. The engines of the hover sputtered. If he chose to aid the gravity stone, they'd all be fine in the event of a crash, but if he proved he could overcome both their wills at once, they'd know he could just as easily convince the granite marble providing gravity for the hover to let them splatter like rotten tomatoes.

"We agree, you go back shackled!" Slater blurted.

"And she comes with us the whole way. Released when you're locked up."

The ground was rushing up fast.

"Deal."

The hover leveled out and parked on solid ground. Snow caught the pilot by the shoulder. "Bring us to wherever they've got Jessie Ramsey stashed."

Eric breathed a sigh of relief.

"Where's that?" the pilot inquired.

Slater waggled his fingers at the hover's controls. "Use the thingie. Figure it out. And make it snappy."

This hadn't been the exact way Plan K was plotted out, but it had worked, nonetheless. Sacrificing himself had been a concession he was willing to make.

After all, she'd done the same for him.

———

A lone traveler saw the line for customs at Discovery Memorial Starport and dodged around it. Well-dressed arriving passengers opted for the priority line, where money could buy back time that might otherwise be wasted queuing with the masses. But the traveler bypassed that group as well.

She was pale and gangly, sporting sandy blonde bangs and a ponytail hidden beneath the hood of her unzipped light jacket. The rest of her outfit consisted of a white tank top, baggy black slacks, and a pair of pristine white tennis shoes. While she might otherwise have been dismissed as an athleisure fan dressing twenty years too young, a pair of gold wire-rimmed spectacles perched on her nose, lending a whiff of sophistication. In one hand, she clutched the straps of a beat-up duffel bag as her only luggage.

A security guard stepped into her path.

She didn't hesitate, bringing up her free hand and flashing the M of the Martian Circle.

The guard backed away with a deferential nod.

Off to the side of the customs zone was a little-used counter attended by a wizard and two tech liaisons, currently engaged in what appeared to be an intense game of gin rummy. One of the techs nudged the wizard with an elbow, a sure sign that this guy was a nobody. It was one thing being nice to the science dudes, another to let them get touchy.

"Name?"

"Going to decline."

The wizard blinked his surprise. "I don't think the question is optional."

"Were you not informed of an anonymous arrival today?" The wizard shook his head. "Well, let's not make that my problem."

The traveler moved to walk past the checkpoint, but the wizard rushed out from behind his counter to block her way. "I have a duty. If I don't have instruction to allow you through, you need to go through the normal process."

She peered through the lenses of her spectacles at him. He was a head taller than her and outweighed her by an even greater margin, yet the lenses were for *his* protection, not hers. She studied the guy who felt entitled to get in her way and decided he wasn't worth bullying with anything more than words.

"Bell."

"Excuse me?"

"You wanted a name. Tiffany Bell."

The wizard slunk back behind his counter. "Sorry, ma'am."

"Damn right, you're sorry. I expect you to keep that info to yourselves. We done here?"

In a tiny voice, the customs wizard added, "Business on Mars?"

She didn't flinch. "I'm here to kill some people. Non-wizards. And not you two chucklefucks, so keep it in your bladders."

The wizard blanched. His lips moved to ask follow-up questions, but no sound came out.

"Whatever you're trying to ask, the answer's above your pay grade. If anyone's got a problem with a bunch of scientists getting their hearts weighed, who exactly are they going to send to deal with it?"

None of them said it, but they knew the answer: either Tiffany or one of a vanishingly small number of her colleagues.

"Um, can I pilot you anywhere?" one of the techs offered. "Or secure local transport?"

Tiffany paused briefly. "Yeah. Code to your ride."

"Excuse me? You have a pilot?" The tech looked past her.

"Yeah. She's wearing my shoes. Flew here from the borderlands. Now, you gonna cough up a code and a landing yard number, or am I going to have to take a fucking taxi?"

Ten minutes later, Tiffany ditched the Martian Circle's courtesy hover two blocks from an unassuming building nestled in the downtown industrial district of New Singapore. Its neighbors were food processing plants and manufacturing for a toy company.

Not everyone knew that this was where Mars Navy kept a planetside prisoner detention and intelligence analysis center. Technically, what Tiffany was planning here was treason, but that presupposed that she cared. It wasn't like she was *from* Mars. The Martian Alliance of Represented Systems was just the lesser evil these days.

Family mattered more than political lines squiggled on a galactic map. And while she barely knew Jessie Ramsey, Esper was the girl's godmother. Some people just needed to be taught the hard way that certain people in this galaxy were looked after.

A guardian angel might have saved Jessie Ramsey from getting caught in the first place. Tiffany was the other sort.

She strode up to the front desk, where an ensign minded a scanner that beeped as navy officers entered and exited the facility. "Excuse me. I'm looking for where new prisoners are kept."

"I'm sorry, ma'am, I... can't... do..." He trailed off, jaw slack, eyes heavy-lidded but unable to close.

Tiffany pushed her spectacles back up and broke eye contact. "Thanks. I'll find my own way." She took the ensign's hand and jammed his thumb against the pad of his own scanner.

The door behind him buzzed, and Tiffany stepped through.

If any of the personnel in the top secret facility objected to Tiffany's presence, she manually altered their opinions.

A lieutenant commander operated the lift for her, punching in his security code to allow access to the priority prisoner level.

Down at the lowest sub-basement, a confused officer took his lift ride back up, unsure why he'd hit the wrong floor.

Getting in was, relatively speaking, the easy part. Whatever wards and alarms the prison had in place would be focused on the prisoner herself. Depending on how long they planned on keeping her, they might have tattooed runes into her skin, embedded a gem in her skull, bound her blood to an object in her cell, or any number of other insidious, less-than-moral means of tracking and controlling her.

Thus far, everything was feeling fairly scientific. If this was the best the Martian Circle could muster for magical defenses around a priority site, Earth was going to eat them alive in covert magical operations.

"Who the hell are you?" a voice demanded.

"I'm looking for Jessie Ramsey," Tiffany replied calmly. Until Mars Navy's wizards showed up, she was free to talk to anyone she liked and just vaporize memories in her wake.

The speaker was a navy commander with a nameplate that read Chowaniec. He had a blaster out and aimed Tiffany's way, showing off admirable reflexes. "I'll ask again, who are you, and how did you get in here?"

He seemed like he ought to know what was going on around here, given his rank and quickness to hold someone at blasterpoint to defend the site's top prisoner.

"You've got five seconds to tell me where Jessie Ramsey is, or I have them put 'too dumb to live' on your tombstone."

Despite decades of military training, Commander Chowaniec faltered. "Your people already picked her up." He angled his torso and shifted his feet, holding his non-blaster arm close to his body as if it was a liability in a fight.

"My people?" Tiffany had to tread carefully around that sort of question. First off, Jimmy Rucker wasn't "her people," and if this guy was on the Rucker Initiative payroll, he had some serious people skills training to brush up on.

"Martian Circle. That's the only way you could have gotten down here without my knowing about it."

"Who took her? Where?"

"Jesus. You people need to get your shit in order."

Tiffany closed the distance in three quick strides. She dropped her duffel, slapped aside Chowaniec's blaster, and drove him up against the wall. "So do yours."

Peering over the lenses of her spectacles, Tiffany extracted the man's memories of the prisoner transfer. Jessie was marched out a rooftop exit under guard and handed over to a pair of robed nobodies with a tech liaison hover. Using the skyscrapers as a rudimentary sundial, she estimated the scene had taken place no more than half an hour before her arrival.

In case she needed any details, she took the memory with her, leaving Chowaniec reeling and dazed and probably still thinking he was keeping Jessie Ramsey in a cell around here somewhere.

It wasn't until she was on her way back to the lift to resume her search topside that Tiffany finally ran into a Martian Circle representative.

"Can I help you?" the older gentleman in the slate gray robes asked pointedly.

"You can forget I was here on your own," Tiffany snapped as she stormed past him. "Save me the trouble."

<hr />

Jessie sat in her cell, both wishing she had access to a chrono and silently thankful she didn't. Much as the handbook said that disorienting a prisoner was a key step in breaking them down, she'd always considered a chrono that displayed seconds to be the worst single companion for captivity.

As her mind wandered in efforts to stave off boredom and torpor, Jessie considered whether the Mars Navy code of justice ought to have specified that shoes be provided to prisoners.

Would Earth Navy be willing to negotiate to get her back?

The coolness in the cell seemed calibrated to teeter her on the verge of needing to shiver.

How dirty and grimy would she have to get before they insisted on giving her clean clothes?

The whole ceiling glowed. Staring straight up seared a floating blur into her retinas, just like glancing at a star while planetside.

Everything but her was gleaming clean. Would they clean

the place every time she was gone? She considered spitting on the wall to test that theory.

Jessie drummed on the edge of the cot as she sat on it, feeling out a rhythm. Composing music wasn't her forte, but it was something she could do entirely in her mind.

This was Day One. As long as she could keep accurate track, she'd mark the days of her confinement.

"Hands on the wall."

Had it been four hours already? She hadn't even attempted to sleep, exhausted in body but not mind.

A faint electronic ping sounded behind her. It repeated roughly once a second. She looked back and spotted a pair of black circles on the wall. The interior of the circles blinked yellow in time with the chime, each large enough for a hand.

Eyes heavy, Jessie blew a sigh. "Make me."

"Fuck you, Ramsey. You're getting released."

She slumped against the wall. "I'll believe you when I get a change of civilian clothes and a blaster."

The panel obscuring the door sank back and slid aside. One of the guards stepped inside with a pair of mag cuffs.

Wait until he's within arm's reach. Stay limp. Then...

Headbutt to the nose.

Throat punch.

Take mag cuffs.

Kick to the side of the knee.

Beeline to Chowaniec.

He'll raise his hands to guard against a strike.

Go low. Tackle. Groin punch. Grapple while he's disoriented. Leg lock; break his neck.

Search for keycards, data crystals, anything to use in escape efforts.

But it wasn't the time. Jessie hadn't gathered enough information about the facility to risk an escape this early in her incarceration. Besides, they wouldn't suspect she'd given up yet. They'd be vigilant.

The guard came within arm's reach, and Jessie did nothing but glare past him. Chowaniec waited, arms folded, a look on his face like someone was pissing on a Martian flag. Rough hands manhandled Jessie facedown on the cot and cuffed her. She put up a token resistance, mostly to keep the guy from over-tightening the cuffs while her muscles were slack.

Out in the hallway, a female lieutenant carried a bundle of clothes and a pair of shoes.

"The fuck is this?"

"Like I said, you're being released."

Jessie wasn't sure what game they were playing. Only Esper had the kind of pull to make this happen, and even that might have been giving the zillionaire wizard too much credit. This wasn't just a political issue, it was also military and magical. In short, considering the shit Jessie was messed up in, it would be criminally negligent to let her loose.

"I don't get it. You can't expect me to fall for this."

Chowaniec pushed the lieutenant forward. "Get her dressed. If you have to, beat her unconscious and do it yourself."

There it was. Jessie caught it in the commander's voice.

Fear.

"Who the hell are you turning me over to?"

"The Martian Circle."

"I'll stay. Thanks." Jessie attempted to back into her cell but a wall of marine corporal blocked her way.

"Have a little self-respect," Chowaniec chided her. Pretty lame put-down, considering it might be his parting shot at her. Another sign he wasn't on his game.

With the guard at her back, Jessie knew she had to act now if she stood a chance. She sprang up and back. A sharp blow to the top of her skull dazed her, but she heard the crack of the guard's jaw. As the grip on her went slack, she twisted and caught him with a knee to the side of the head as he collapsed unconscious.

Jessie dropped to the ground and swept Chowaniec's legs out from under him.

The guard's thumb scan released the mag cuffs, even limp.

Chowaniec scrambled to his feet, but Jessie got to him before he got his balance, dragging him back to the floor.

Arms and legs tangled. Chowaniec was stronger, but he lacked her hand-to-hand combat training. Jessie used a combination of leverage and quick, disorienting strikes to outgrapple the Mars Navy interrogator, catching him in an arm bar and breaking bones.

While she hadn't intervened directly, the lieutenant hadn't been idle. "Suppression team to max security. This is not a drill. Repeat. Suppression team to max security *on the double*. This is not a drill."

With a broken arm, Chowaniec didn't stand a chance, and Jessie didn't have time to break every other bone in his body. Rolling upright, she spared an elbow to shatter his nose, but then her attention turned to the lone other Mars Navy officer on the scene.

Security protocols seemed to have barred weapons on the guards and personnel visiting this level. The lieutenant had nothing apparent to steal in terms of weapons. All she had was a change of clothes and her own uniform. The former would be an upgrade over her prisoner jumpsuit; the latter would be a pain in the ass to steal on short notice but might buy enough confusion to escape.

Despite this being a prison, the lift still had a floor indicator. There was a lift car coming down, and it was the timer until Jessie needed to be ready to fight again.

Time to make quick work of an obvious caffeine logistics officer.

The lieutenant let out a yip as Jessie rushed her and dropped the bundle of civilian clothes. She backed away, turned to run.

Jessie slammed into her from behind. They crashed into a wall. In seconds, Jessie had one arm around the woman's neck, the other wrenched an arm behind her back, steering her like a grav sled toward the lift.

She'd done this from the other side. Squad work. Clearing a building. That lift was a fortress coming down, and the number of guys inside would equal the number of blaster rifles she'd be staring down the instant those doors opened.

Using her captive lieutenant as a battering ram, Jessie charged the door.

"No-no-no-no-no-no," the lieutenant pleaded.

The lift doors slid open. Jessie charged straight in. A hail of startled blaster fire hammered in.

In tight quarters, Jessie found herself outnumbered six to one by marine guards in riot armor. One arm went numb from a collateral stun blast as her captive turned into a convulsing wreck of misfiring muscular nerves. Jessie grabbed for the nearest blaster rifle.

The fact she was in the midst of the suppression team kept them from bringing their blasters to bear. The only one safe to fire at will was her. Anyone else was far more likely to hit a friendly target.

But that was as far as the plan got.

With one arm tingling and slow to respond, Jessie wasn't able to wrest even a single weapon away from the response team.

Fists, elbows, and rifle butts hammered the consciousness out of her.

When Jessie came to, she ached all over. A piece of gauze blocked one nostril, and her left eye was swollen shut. She was dressed, including shoes, but detailed exploration of both her medical condition and her wardrobe was impeded by two key facts.

One: she was mag-cuffed again.

Two: a pair of marines were carrying her by the upper arms toward a waiting hover.

A wave of dizziness washed over her—likely aftereffects of her concussion—as she raised her head. Late evening sunlight stabbed her eyes.

The hover pilot came around and opened the door.

A wizard stepped out.

Then another.

Existential dread curdled the contents of Jessie's stomach. What did the Martian Circle want from her that they were willing to strongarm Mars Navy to get? Nothing good, that was for damn sure.

But as her turbulent thoughts settled, Jessie realized that she recognized those wizards.

Wizard Snow and Wizard Slater.

Then, Eric waved from inside the passenger compartment.

What was going on here?

"Eric, what did you do?" she demanded as the marines stuffed her into the back of the hover. She had to clench her jaw as she spoke, since moving it hurt.

The two wizards crowded back into the hover. It was a larger model limousine-style ride, with forward- and rearward-facing bench seats. She and Eric faced Eric's parole officers.

"Are you all right?" Eric asked, leaning forward and looking up at her nose. "I thought science usually did better at crash injuries."

Since Eric wasn't being any help, she addressed her

question to Wizard Slater. "What kind of deal did he cut?"

———

Eric fretted in his seat. Jessie was confused right now, and this was just the reprieve before she got furious.

"Simple matter," Wizard Slater replied to his sister's request for answers. "Your brother has offered his cooperation in return for your release."

"ASSHOLE!" Jessie screamed at him. "After all I did to make sure we didn't *both* get caught, and you went and turned yourself in?"

"They caught me."

"Caught you..." Jessie echoed. He nodded meekly. "Despite the fact you can apparently snap together a convincing disguise in a... well, a snap?"

Eric gave her shoulder a gingerly pat. "You're not tip-top right now. I can overlook the awkward phraseology. But couldn't let them dissect you or turn you into a chemical-fueled monster or whatever."

"One small matter," Wizard Snow cut in.

He produced a small wooden case. And held it out toward Eric. This was his payment.

Jessie wasn't willing to remain silent for what ought to have been a solemn moment. "What's going on? What's in there? An oath demon? Soul crystal?"

When the lid opened, the contents were far less interesting. Frankly, Eric wouldn't have minded meeting an oath demon. He'd have pledged quite a bit to sort out this mess a little less messily. A short length of chain joined a pair of silver bracelets opened like the pincers of a crab. Runes shouted obscenities across the surface; they might have been pretty had Eric not understood the message they were broadcasting.

Hopelessness.

Confinement.

Servitude.

"Don't you dare!"

"Only one of us caused this mess. It's bad enough I stole five years from you. I can't let you get punished on top of that." He held out his wrists.

Wizard Snow shook his head and twirled a finger. Eric sighed and turned around. It was awkward since seats were meant to support a human body in one particular direction but not the exact opposite. He winced as the arcane shackles bit into his wrists, burrowing metal barbs into bones and veins. "Ow!"

"Idiot..."

Wizard Snow slouched back in his seat and exchanged a fist bump with his partner. "Thus ends the longest assignment ever."

"I'll feel better when the council accepts our final report," Wizard Slater replied.

"I'm really sorry, guys," Eric told them as he tried to find a comfortable position sitting while unable to use the back rest without crushing his own hands.

"Don't apologize to these fucks," Jessie ordered, then, noticing his predicament, added, "You can't find a comfortable way to sit. Get used to it; they're *designed* to be uncomfortable."

Hah. He bet *her* shackles weren't trying to wrap themselves around her blood vessels and burrow for bone marrow. But that would just make her feel worse if he mentioned it. It wasn't an argument worth winning.

"Don't worry," Wizard Snow offered. "We don't care one whit about you. We'll find someone to get you off Mars and into neutral territory. Unwitting passenger in an unsanctioned temporo-magical excursion. Pre-date the current civil war, so we officially recognize you as a non-combatant. PR folks'll dress it up nicer, but that'll be the gist."

"We're really not the enemy here," Slater tried to assure her.

"You maybe need to work a little closer with the PR team, then, since you sure seem to be doing everything enemy-style here."

"He's dangerous, you know."

Eric hung his head.

"We're protecting the galaxy from him."

Eric slumped sideways, leaning against the window as New Singapore flew by below them.

"Imagine if it had been that whole restaurant, not just the two of you?"

"Or the whole city?"

Jessie scowled. "Was that even a possibility?"

"You have no idea how powerful your brother is."

"And reckless."

"Unfocused, I'd call it."

"Hey. I mean, he's on a little different frequency than the rest of us," Jessie said, coming to his defense. "But I always figured that was just a wizard being a wizard. Seems a little disrespectful stomping him when he's given you everything you wanted."

"Two promotions and five years of being the butt of time travel jokes?" Snow countered.

Slater nodded in solidarity. "Missed a grandson being born during all those inquests."

"Sorry," Eric murmured.

Jessie rammed a shoulder into him. "Stop apologizing to these assholes!" She looked out her own window. "Where are you even taking us?"

"We need to bring Eric in. Once he's safely out of public

life, there will be no further reason to keep you. Damien here will then take you to the nearest starport and get you on a ship leaving Mars."

"Hi," Damien called out from the front seat, offering the silhouette of a wave.

Eric squirmed again, more uncomfortable with the conversation than with the shackles he was being forced to endure—not that those weren't also a downer.

"Can't you guys just stop?" he whined.

"Sorry," Snow replied smugly. "You don't get to dictate terms anymore. We met your one demand. I'd like to see you *try* to crash the hover with those on."

Jessie fixed a look at him like he'd never seen before. "You threatened to cut the science and kill them in a hover crash?"

Already condemned, there was no reason to deny it. "Yeah. And keep the gravity stone from saving us."

"But there's two of them."

Slater snickered. "We told you, he's more dangerous than you realized."

"Not anymore," Snow amended with a pedantic finger raised.

"You could have overpowered two of them?"

Eric swallowed, then nodded.

Jessie's gaze wandered down to Eric's lap. She looked back up. "Weren't those shackles behind your back a second ago?"

Eric looked down, too. Somehow, he'd barely registered that he'd settled in properly on the seat. Now it made sense how.

"Huh. Would you look at that?"

Across the passenger cabin of the Martian Circle's limousine, Snow and Slater exchanged a wide-eyed look.

Jessie stared, struggling to consider the ramifications of her brother having his hands in front of him. It wasn't that it improved his skills as a combatant. He had none. And as best she knew, hand position didn't matter except for wizards who were into that whole finger-twiddling kind of magic.

But his hands had been trapped behind him.

Eric was no contortionist. If he'd even tried slipping his feet through, everyone would have noticed as he kicked, elbowed, and shoulder-checked everyone in the process. So, either he'd been doing yoga since getting kicked out of school, the chain of those shackles was made of elastic, or he'd used magic with no one even noticing—including himself.

"Tell me you can't just work any goddamn magic you please."

"He can't," Snow chimed in. "The shackles use an ancient formula for canceling the wearer's connection to the universal ear."

Jessie glanced back at the shackles, now in plain view as Eric rested his wrists in his lap. Her implication didn't sneak past the wizards.

"It's a street performer's trick," Slater assured her. "Many disgraced wizards turn to prestidigitation as a harmless hobby."

"Eriiiiic. If you can take these guys, say so."

"I wouldn't push my luck if I were you," Wizard Snow warned with a paternal sort of menace.

"Luck is resourcefulness plus courage," Jessie said, but she was ignoring the Martian Circle assholes and addressing Eric solely. Mom always believed in making her own luck. It had seen her through the Typhoon combat in three different wars. Jessie hoped they could make enough now to get out of a hover with two bureaucratic wizards.

"Take a win when you get it." Slater sounded nervous.

"You're relying on our largess now that Eric's been muzzled." That was false bluster.

Dammit. "You didn't give up on me. I'm not willing to leave you to these assholes!"

"Hey! Let your brother be!"

"Quiet, or we may be forced to quiet you!"

"ERIC!"

Eric shook his head. "I don't want to hurt anyone."

"Do we... uh... need a safety landing?" the pilot asked.

"Keep flying!" Snow insisted.

A cold calm settled over Jessie as a course of action became clear.

Springing into motion, she lunged for Wizard Snow, feet first. In the limousine cabin, there wasn't a lot of room to maneuver, much less dodge. And generally, any self-respecting wizard would think to defend themselves with magic.

The blow struck with a crack. Snow's head snapped back, blinking and dazed.

Slater gestured toward Jessie with the sort of motion that might have looked right if lightning shot out at the end, but it ended up looking like a holo shoot before the effects guys added the magic. Instead, she made a fool of herself.

Under less desperate circumstances, Jessie might have appreciated the comical brawl that ensued. Snow was twice her size but with muscles hard as a gymnastics mat. Slater had the kind of physique maintained by extensive walking and never lifting anything heavier than a beverage. They flailed and batted and slapped and grabbed. In return, even with her arms still trapped by the mag cuffs behind her back, Jessie gave an anatomy lesson in pain, pressure points, and the break strength of human bones. She fought with feet and knees, shoulders, and her own skull.

With Slater limp and drooling blood on the limousine floor,

Jessie eventually got her hands involved, maneuvering back-to-back with Snow. From her position on top, she used her shackled wrists in a guillotine choke hold.

Oh, it was tempting to use the unyielding metal cuffs to crush his windpipe and let him suffocate. Instead, she used pressure on his carotid to cut off the oxygen to his weaponized wizard brain.

As soon as the heavier wizard slumped onto the seat out cold, a yelp from the cockpit signaled the pilot's realization that the prisoners had succeeded in overpowering his wizard superiors.

With a whirr, a divider rose to separate the passengers from the cockpit.

Reacting without hesitation, Jessie got her feet under her and dove, trampling her brother in the process. She managed to get her head through before the gap narrowed to shut her out.

The divider came up and caught her neck.

Then the divider paused and quickly reversed.

"Safety feature," Jessie informed the pilot. "It's a limo. The VIPs are the ones who get protected."

"Please don't hurt me!"

"Are they dead?" Eric asked.

"No one's dead. No one's *getting* dead. Not if you play ball, Damien. *Intelligas?*"

Damien the pilot nodded frantically.

Jessie slid back into the passenger compartment. "Can you get rid of these?"

Suddenly, Jessie's hands were free. She shook the sensation back into her fingers, feeling every fresh bruise and potentially cracked bone in her body in the process. Her adrenaline high was starting to wear off, allowing all her injuries to report in with requests for treatment.

She pawed around on the seat behind her, then turned to

search visually. "Where'd they go?" If Eric hadn't fucked them up too bad, she figured the mag cuffs could delay the pilot going for help without having to hurt him too badly.

"You didn't specify," Eric replied. "I don't know whether they exist or went somewhere else or turned into air. I really wasn't planning on keeping souvenirs."

"You're talkative now that these two fuckers have a boxer's hangover."

"They're scary."

Jessie grabbed a handful of Snow's hair and pulled his head up. "You did this. *We* did this. Stick together, and maybe we'll get off this miserable, overpopulated 3-ball."

"We're the good guys," Damien protested, distress clear from the sniffles between words.

"It *is* a nice planet when people aren't chasing you or arresting you or threatening to keep your eyeballs in a jar."

Jessie cringed. "Is that what they had in store for you?"

"Just guessing from Uncle Enzio's stories. *They* were pretty vague."

"Um. Where are we heading?" Damien inquired. "I'm just sticking to our current travel lane and maintaining an inconspicuous speed."

God, Jessie wished she had tech liaisons in her job. They were obsequious to a fault. As a hostage, Damien ought to have been doing everything in his power to draw the attention of law enforcement without Jessie or Eric noticing.

"Where were we heading before?" Jessie asked.

"Discovery Memorial."

"We should pick a different starport," Eric advised. It was, at a basic level, sound planning.

It would also have been an early warning that there had been a change of plans. Even if Damien was totally going to play ball, she couldn't trust that quiver in his voice if someone raised him on a comm, and if whoever checked in on them wanted to hear from the napping wizards, the chase would be on.

"No. Same plan. Head for the passenger dropoff at Discovery Memorial."

Jessie rubbed a hand over her jaw, idly taking stock of potential needs for dental care. At the same time, she pondered the fates of the wizards.

Killing them was sorely tempting. But if they ever wanted sympathy from the Martian Alliance of Represented Systems, they couldn't go offing unconscious wizards. She mused aloud, "What do we do with you two...?"

Eric leaned down and clamped his shackles around one of Snow's wrists and one of Slater's. "That ought to flummox them pretty good."

Jessie chuckled and shook her head. "With how easy those come off, I don't know how much use they'll be."

"I may not be an expert," Damien called back to them. "But those magic handcuffs aren't supposed to be able to be removed without some special wand or something they keep at the detention center. Wizards Snow and Slater *assured* me you'd be harmless."

Eric just shrugged.

It wasn't a long trip to Discovery Memorial Starport.

"Private dropoff, not whichever one the wizards use," Jessie instructed as they descended for a landing. "Depending how many people are paying attention, we could be on a short chrono from there."

"Thank you for the ride," Eric added cheerfully as the starport passenger exchange area rose up around them.

Jessie rifled through the wizards' pockets but didn't come up with anything that might prove last-second useful.

Well, flying commercial had always been off the table.

Without cash or barter for a bribe, booking the Shady Express off Mars wasn't happening either.

That left three options, stowing away, storming a ship, or signing on as crew.

The hover touched down with maybe more of a thud than a pilot with his head screwed on right would have allowed. But Jessie was willing to cut Damien a little slack.

Door locks clunked open. Jessie hopped out, scanning the area for anyone suspicious. No one but her and Eric triggered that sixth sense she'd honed.

"Take me with you," Damien pleaded from the pilot door's open window.

Jessie froze.

No.

This wasn't happening.

They weren't taking in a stray tech liaison just because someone might catch consequences for helping them.

"Eric..."

Her brother sighed. "I'll do what I can."

"Make it quick. I'm going to scout out the independent landing yard."

Jessie barely dared let Eric out of her sight, but they couldn't leave a loose end with his memory intact, and she couldn't just stand there doing nothing.

▭

"Have you ever had your memory wiped before?" Eric asked with all the bedside manner he could muster.

Poor Damien. He was a mess. Short, shuddering breaths teetered on the verge of becoming sobs at any moment. "How... how would I know?"

It was a good and fair question, and Eric didn't know how

to solve the implied conundrum. "Well, that's neither here nor there. It's not really my area of expertise. Then again, I'm not sure I really *have* an area of expertise, much as I might like to think I do. But really, how complicated could it—?"

"Please, kill me."

The words were a mouse's squeak, but Eric heard them.

"I'm not that kind of wizard."

"Please. I know. You're just in the wrong place at the *very* wrong time. Me too. Except I can't run. I can't stay. They're going to find me, and you don't want to know what they'll do to me."

Eric had his guesses. They were similar to the guesses as to his own fate prior to Jessie taking the steering yoke of his destiny and giving it a hard yank to starboard.

Even if Damien knew nothing, they'd never take him at his word. A Convocation by any other name would take his mind apart like a jigsaw to check for the slightest clue.

He swallowed.

This was never easy.

"I can take you with us."

"Really?" Hope sparked in Damien's tear-glistening eyes. "But your sister said—"

"She doesn't get to know."

Damien shook his head, clearly confused. "I don't understand. How can you hide me?"

"I'll take you away from here, but not the way you're thinking."

"Where?"

Eric gently guided the man's chin. "I'll show you. Look into my eyes."

———

Reality fell away.

Eric was used to the sensation, but Damien needed to scream for a little while to get it out of his system. But sometime around when he needed to refill his lungs with air before a second terrified shriek, the martian tech liaison realized that he wasn't in any pain or real distress.

"Where are we? How did we get here?"

Eric pursed his lips and tried his best to explain. He'd never really been good at salesmanship, so it was a constant struggle. "OK, the answer to your second question is, quite obviously, magic. But would it surprise you to learn that it's also a good answer to the first as well?"

"I... No. I don't think that helps."

Damien's confusion was perfectly understandable. They stood together atop a green knoll whose surface lacked an identifiable substance. It wasn't grass or permacrete, wood or stone. It was merely... green. Down in the valley below, a chessboard pattern spread over an area too large to play a regulation game, where pawns would die of exhaustion before promoting to rooks or queens. The sky was a uniform shade of sunset pink.

In place of clouds, common household objects floated overhead.

Damien took in the sights with the glazed expression of a man who had stopped accepting the possibility that what he saw was real.

"You're in my imagination." It was blunt but true.

"Am I asleep?"

"No. Sleep is a state of unconsciousness. You're conscious."

"Are *you* asleep?"

Eric broke into a grin. "That's a great question! Right now, it's more like a light meditation. But everything is here—

whether I'm awake, asleep, or anywhere in between. Maybe this'll be easier to explain since you work around wizards."

"That's really my current dilemma. Unless you can hide my body in here, too, they're going to find me."

"What is 'me' in this context?" Eric asked. "Hmm? Is it the piece of meat in the seat in that hover you flew us around in? Or is it the part here asking me insightful questions?"

Damien backed away. As he did so, the whole knoll rolled to keep him at the top. Eric kept pace at a leisurely stroll. "You took my mind out of my body."

"Isn't that better than erasing it entirely? A new life. None of the consequences. An endless playground to explore."

Damien shook his head.

Why did they always object?

"Until you get bored or decide hurting me is fun or... or... THIS IS CRAZY!'

This called for the big guns.

Eric lifted both hands, and barks and yips heralded the arrival of a stampede. Damien whirled to face the sound just in time to get swarmed by dozens of tail-wagging puppies, bounding and falling over one another in their eagerness to greet their new friend. Every breed and mix numbered among the herd—all that Eric had heard of at least—just in case Damien was particular about certain pedigrees of companion. Many had multiple representatives, since that was just how the galaxy worked.

"What is this?"

"They're called puppies, just like out there. They want to make friends, since, well, you're new, and that's their first instinct when meeting someone new. Feel free to adopt one or two."

"Are you trying to bribe me into living in your imagination with a puppy?"

Wow. It really was different dealing with a tech liaison. Despite his all-too-common denial of the reality around him, he was quick enough to pick up on the more nuanced aspects.

"I'm making the case that you can be happy here. I don't know what you had going on out there—"

"Working for the Martian Circle was my life!"

Eric let out a breath he'd been holding in reserve. "Well, that's a relief. Nothing sadder than turning into a job. I'll posit this to you: The Martian Circle took over your life and had you running around flying bullies all over Mars. Probably a bunch of other menial tasks. There's nothing wrong with honest work. But you let them turn it into everything. I'm at least being up front that I control this world, and I'll host a life that will be way more fulfilling."

"There is no meaning without sentient connection. And let's be honest, I don't know that I want to be with *just you* for the rest of my life."

Eric's gotcha grin was the first tip of his hand that he'd won Damien over. "Come with me."

A bicycle flew up, towing a park bench behind it. Eric took a seat, and a reluctant Damien followed suit.

They whooshed into the pink sky, passing toothbrushes, laser hair trimmers, refrigerators, and all other manner of devices. He caught Damien staring in a mixture of confusion and existential horror. One of these days, Eric was going to have to find another place to do this. For him, it was a cultural reminder of the scientific world his body lived in. In the meantime, Eric brought them down in a town square.

If one were disinclined to gaze upward, one might have mistaken the square for part of a Victorian theme park. Dignified brick buildings stretched several stories tall, surrounding a cobblestone plaza with a fountain at its center.

The bench landed within comfortable enjoying range of

the fountain, and the bicycle took off without it.

"Are you... going to turn me into a fountain?" Damien asked, still clearly struggling with the metaphysics at work. He pointed up at the generic humanoid statue at the fountain's center, devoid of features and simpler than the most basic mannequin, made of circles and ovals.

"No. That's just a representation of potential. It's nobody, but it could become anyone." Eric smiled. "Just like you."

"I don't understand."

That much was obvious. Luckily, Eric had help.

Around the square, the buildings carried categorical names, including "Places," "Stuff," "Concepts," and most importantly, "People."

From the People building came a woman in a slim blue dress and beehive hairdo, high-heeled boots clacking on the cobbles.

"Damien, I'd like you to meet Uriela. She's sort of the welcome committee."

She looked like the curtseying sort, until you got to know her, but Uriela offered a handshake, which a baffled Damien accepted.

"A pleasure." She turned to Eric. "A new arrival or a guest?"

"He hasn't decided yet."

Uriela folded her arms. "What's the problem? Religious, suspicious, or clingy?"

"Last two, I think. Haven't noticed any praying."

"Is praying required?" Damien asked.

Eric imagined the bench a little wider, and Uriela joined them, bracketing Damien on the far side.

"It's not," Eric assured him. "But I find that most believers try praying their way somewhere else—not that there's anything wrong with here," he amended hastily.

"Can you please stop talking, sir?" Uriela asked. "Just for a little bit."

Eric nodded.

"Damien, what's your problem out there?"

"How do you know there's a problem?"

Uriela smirked. "No one comes here if everything is hunky dory out there. It's fine to talk about it. Everyone has a story."

"What's yours?"

"I was one hundred and thirty-seven years old, and more machines and tubes than person."

Damien blinked and took another look at her. Uriela was pretty and maybe thirty going strictly by visual cues. Of course, appearances didn't matter here.

"And you?" she prompted.

"I work for the Martian Circle. That's like... Mars's version of the Convocation. We're at war now. But I helped Eric and his sister."

"Ah. Your own people are coming for you."

"Is... that common? It's a weird thing to guess."

"You're not the first refugee from the consequences of doing the right thing. Come on. Let go. You might not believe it yet, but today was your lucky day."

Damien looked to the sky. "I'm not sure I like it here." A plasma welder tumbled by overhead.

Uriela burst out laughing. "You're not the only one. This place is weird. But it's Eric's jam. We'll find you somewhere that feels right for you."

"There are other parts of this wonderland?"

"Plenty!" Eric chimed in. "Oh, we have everything in here. Well, not everything. That's a work in progress. But there are cities, countryside, moons, asteroids, boats, starships, beaches, mountains. If it's not here, I can make it custom."

"Think of this place as a theme park," Uriela suggested.

Damien nodded along, finally seeming to understand at least the basics. It was time to close the deal.

Eric stood and spread his arms. "Welcome to the Village of Eternity, where the theme is reincarnation!"

<hr />

Jessie leaned against a structural support pillar, watching the foot traffic in the public access area of the Discovery Memorial landing yard. Medium and solo-class transports and micro-freighters parked around the interior of the open, cylindrical structure, with a regular stream of vessels filtering in and out. None of them were good candidates for an escape. The departures were obvious misses; the ones just arriving wouldn't be leaving soon enough for her liking.

Mars was a neutron anti-personnel mine, and Jessie had touched the trigger. Defusing it would be a delicate operation; the explosion could come without warning or hope of survival.

Footsteps always warranted a glance, no matter the number of Martians milling around. Looking suspicious as hell was a sacrifice and a tradeoff. Jessie was ever so much more guilty than hell. When she checked, a tentative wave announced Eric's arrival.

She kept her voice low as her brother crept up beside her. "That was quick. You sure you got everything?" Last thing she needed was a sloppy, amateur mind wipe turning into an instant liability.

"Nothing to worry about," Eric replied cheerily but with the good sense to stay quiet about it. He peered all around. "Which one are we going to fly away on?"

"Wish I had an answer. Still looking."

Their ideal ride was a captain-only vessel, looking more

reputable than it might really be, in good repair, and ready to depart.

Eric whispered his question in her ear. "What are we looking for?"

"A diamond in the coal pile. We only get one shot. Fuck this up, and we're back to shackles. Any chance you could magic us up some disguises?"

"Not if we don't want to get noticed. I was in a kid's body when they sniffed me out. Big starport like this will have real wizards around and detectors. So much tech. SOOO much tech. They can't let people run around making magic."

It was a fair point. Commercial star travel would have ground to a halt centuries ago if wizards used magic in starports.

"Worse comes to worst, you willing to fight to stay out of custody?" Much as she was up on her feet, Jessie wasn't feeling like another brawl. Every bone in her body ached and would continue to do so until she got some medical attention.

"There are worse things than prison."

"Don't count on that." Jessie didn't relish Chowaniec getting her back in a cell, on his schedule, playing his games. She let out a groan as her jaw protested the amount of talking she was subjecting it to.

"Are you ok?"

Much as it stabbed her in the ribs, Jessie couldn't suppress a chuckle. "Are you just noticing?"

"It's rude to ask tough people that. I'd been trying *not* to be rude, but you *do* look pretty bad."

"I'll live."

"Should we find a hospital ship?" Eric craned his neck like he expected to find one parked in the private lot at Discovery Memorial.

"Anyone passing a ship inspection's got a med kit on board.

That'll do." A bone knitter and some analgesics. That's all she needed. She probably looked worse than she really felt.

A dawning realization made her blink; there was an asset she'd been overlooking.

"Oh! You had an idea! I saw it! Your eyes did the thing. What is it? Did you figure out a way to buy a new starship with a fake ID and flying it off while you're taking a test flight?"

"How oddly specific. No. But we've got a cover story."

"Who am I?" Eric asked with giddy excitement.

"My brother."

He scowled. "Not much of a story."

"Best stories—"

"Are true except where you need them not to be," Eric quoted dutifully.

"You got me out of a bad situation. We're looking to get away from a boyfriend."

"Yours or mine?"

"Mine."

"'K."

"We're willing to go anywhere he's going. Long as it's not Mars."

"He has to be a 'he'?"

Jessie paused to consider. A woman might be more sympathetic. Then again, a woman might also pick up on emotional details that Jessie wasn't equipped to fake. She also might notice that several of Jessie's injuries weren't entirely defensive in nature. And if she noticed the telltale chafing from cuffs, it might be hard not to get the authorities dragged into this.

"Let's try for a guy."

"How much story goes with this? Did I rush in heroically, sneak you out a back door...?"

"Minimal detail. If we get aboard and get found out, we

switch to a hijacking. Got it?"

The scramble to get out of the system would be harrowing if anything went wrong outbound. A wrong transit code, surprise customs check, their ride having a warrant of its own spring up out of nowhere, or the captain just getting suspicious while he still had access to a comm.

"Remember Uncle Roddy's old story about Mort doing a wizard astral drop? So deep the astral changed color?"

"Sure," Eric replied with a shrug.

"Things get bad, think you can pull off the same trick?"

Again, Eric shrugged. "I assume so."

"Assume..."

"People don't just let you practice that sort of thing. Everyone's all 'we'd all die without oxygen' or 'you'd dump us in an alternate reality' when you bring it up. But I'm willing to give it a try."

"Fine. Consider that our Plan B."

"L."

"Huh?"

"Just getting this far was Plan K. Actually, if you had a series of lettered plans, should we combine our lettering in series or parallel? Were you past K already, or were we just starting at A again because you'd been working without a plan?"

"L is fine," Jessie replied, sidestepping the whole argument.

Her eyes hadn't been idle as they chattered. Second level, far side of the cylinder, a lone starship captain had just slammed closed the hatch after swapping out fuel rods. That didn't mean he was planning on lifting off right this minute, but it ought to have meant he'd be able to if he wanted.

Without binocs, she couldn't tell much about the captain. Human. Probably male. Didn't see any other crew. Ship wasn't huge. It would do.

"Follow me."

Eric, if nothing else, could follow direction without asking a million questions when the time came. He fell in like a puppy behind her and a step to her left.

Silos like this made up half the private side of the starport. That didn't mean the amenities were great. Mars was nearly as old as Earth at this point. Not wanting to take a lift and risk the kind of conversations that popped up in closed quarters with nosy strangers, Jessie found the open stairwell that spiralled up from level to level of the structure.

Her ribs voted for the lift but lost in a close decision. Had there been another two or three levels to go, maybe there would have been another outcome, but Jessie made it to the top, gasping for breath since she'd been trying to avoid breathing at all as she ascended.

"You're in worse shape than you're willing to admit."

"I'm fine."

"Liar."

"I'm fine *enough*. Let me do the talking."

"I hate that phrase."

"PLEASE."

Eric clamped his mouth shut, but she could tell he didn't like it.

They reached the vessel she'd picked out. It was a Condor Mk 4, maybe twenty years old. Pockmarked tint job from flying in borderspace with no orbital cleansing. The name on the side identified it as *Kierkegaard*.

"Excuse me," Jessie called out. She left her jaw clenched even though her teeth didn't feel quite as loose as they had earlier. "Are you the captain of this ship?"

A head ducked out of the open boarding ramp. "Oh. Hello. That's me, Captain Lorenzo Byron. What're you two selling?" he asked sarcastically, grinning with a gleaming white smile

Captain Byron cut a dashing figure with a square jaw and a shading of stubble. He wasn't jacked but had a trim and athletic build. He wore a mechanic's jumpsuit with the top dangling loose above the belt. He was covered in sweat that had soaked the tank top beneath. He wiped his forehead with the back of a work glove.

"Looking for a quick ride off Mars."

"Flat fee. Three heavy. Per. Up front."

Oof. Unless inflation had gone crazy or the Martian currency was seriously devalued, this guy was screwing them over.

Not that she had money.

"Please. I'm on the run. My brother got me out of a bad situation."

Captain Byron slouched against the opening of the boarding door. "At least you went with the siblings thing. Good call, considering the family resemblance. That cosmo, or you get someone to hit you?"

"You think we're scamming you?" Jessie demanded. What an asshole. Thus far, she hadn't even lied.

"Oh, I know you're scamming me. I just don't know what scam just yet." He turned to call into his ship. "Figgy, c'mere a sec."

Shit, he wasn't alone, either. "Look, we're not after any trouble." She backed away a step. Pressing her luck wasn't worth the risk. They'd find another ship.

"Sure. Just a free ride." A laaku in a tracksuit, smoking a digital vaporizer, joined Byron in the doorway. "Hey, Figs, girl says she got beat on. Looking for an evac. What you think?"

The laaku muttered something she couldn't understand, though she picked out a couple words of what she thought might be Kejathi.

Eric giggled.

That caught the laaku's ear. "You understand Kejathi?"

Eric rattled off a few sentences. It was Figgy's turn to laugh.

The laaku turned to his partner. "Whaddaya think? Kid seems OK to me."

Byron remained fixed in place, gaze not leaving Jessie. "Make you a deal. You tell me why you're *really* looking for a ride, and I'll take the both of you gratis."

The laaku garbled something.

"Because I'm not convinced she *can* tell the truth."

Eric launched into what sounded like an impassioned speech. Jessie could only pick out maybe five words, all articles and conjunctions.

Byron's expression drifted from suspicious to incredulous to outright amusement.

"You believe a word of this?"

Figgy shrugged. "If you were trying to come up with a lie, would that make it past the brainstorm?"

Eric held up a swearing hand. "All true."

"Why would you tell us all that?"

Jessie leaned into the path to look her brother in the face. "What *did* you tell them?"

"The truth. That we're the most wanted fugitives on Mars, and if we're not spacebound in the next few minutes, we're all dead."

Jessie approached the pair with her hands up. "Look. I know he sounds crazy, but he's really—"

"Very dangerous," Eric cut in. "I like to think that my gregarious nature makes up for the fact, but that's a personal choice. I don't want to hurt anyone, but we really are in a terrible hurry. And the money will be there. I swear."

Figgy puffed on his vape. "Not sure what to believe, but he's threatening to beat us to death with a carrot. Might as well eat it."

Byron stepped aside and swept a hand toward the ship's interior. "How can I resist such eloquent extortion? Welcome aboard the *Kierkegaard*."

As Eric marched past her toward the ship's entrance, he sniped with a quick, "You can do all the talking next time."

The New Singapore Northeast Martian Circle Technical Liaison Outreach Center droned with everyday activity. Wizards, liaisons, and the odd regular, non-magical Martian looking for help with unwelcome magic in her life. The local wizards mostly wore the Mars cut of the traditional occult robe. Liaisons looked sharp in their all-black suits.

Of course, the citizenry dressed however the fuck they felt like. Thus, it might have come as no surprise that Tiffany Bell met an objection when she bypassed the line of petitioning Martians looking for redress of their arcane troubles.

"Excuse me, ma'am, you need to go to the back of that line over there," a senior tech liaison informed her with a wiggling finger aimed past her to where the line formed.

"The only word you got right was 'ma'am,' now scoot." With the flick of a finger, she sent the condescending asshole stumbling aside without touching him. Realizing that she didn't know her way around this particular office, she turned back to the flustered gentleman. "Which way to collections?"

The humbled liaison gulped. "Um. Third floor. Second door on the left."

"Thanks."

Nice place like this, Tiffany expected and was pleased to find a fully magical lift. She rode up with two more liaisons and a bored wizard of an administrative bent. The techs glanced at her duffel but said nothing. It was the wizard who got nosy.

"Whatcha got there? You get displaced in an incident? That all your clothes? We're not all like that, you know. Really very uncommon. Most wizards wouldn't hurt a fly."

"Guess I'm not like most wizards," Tiffany said without looking back as she exited at her floor.

She didn't know how many of her fellow passengers had business on the third floor, but none decided to disembark.

The Collections Department was a nice little euphemism. A wizard at the desk openly read a book and didn't look up until Tiffany dropped her duffel in front of him.

"Can I help you?"

"Got someone on hand who can make digital deposits?" she asked.

"We don't do digital for payouts under five hundred."

"I don't stop into an outreach center for less than fifty heavy."

The collections wizard stiffened. "What are you bringing me? You have information on a most-wanted case?"

Tiffany unzipped the duffel and rummaged through a mixture of dirty and clean laundry. When she found what she was looking for, she dropped a silk bundle on the desk and untied the cord that kept it from falling open in transit.

Her audience watched rapt as she unfolded and unrolled the cloth.

Silver glinted. Tightly packed chains clattered as they gained their freedom.

All six medallions were the same, yet no two *exactly* alike. They differed slightly in size and style, reflecting the personal tastes of their previous owners. But all shared the common shape of a letter "C" being struck through by a bolt of lightning.

"We'll need to verify," the wizard said after working moisture back into his mouth.

"I'm not hanging around here all day. I'll leave my account

info. If I don't see a deposit by tomorrow morning, I'll be back for answers."

After a brief wait, a diligent young man arrived with a pen and paper. "If you can write down your account number here, I'll transcribe it to—"

"Fuck's sake. Take a scan." Tiffany held out a thumb. After fumbling for the device, she pressed her digit to the screen. A beep confirmed it had read her thumbprint successfully. She checked the embroidered name on the liaison's suit. "Great. Now... Clarence, it's you I'll be asking for if my payment doesn't show up. Rate still fifteen per."

"Unless they were high-priority targets."

"Nope. Just run-of-the-mill schmucks today."

Clarence nodded vigorously. "Should be ninety coming to you after the formality of verification. In the meantime, can I arrange lodging for you, someplace for a nice dinner?"

"I'm good, thanks. But that does remind me that I need to make a comm."

Clarence perked right up. "I can handle that for you."

Rolling her eyes, Tiffany yanked her duffel off the counter and reached inside her jacket with her free hand. Her datapad was a kiddie model, clunky and bright pink, adorned with kitty ears. It was fucking adorable. More importantly, it always turned back on after seeing rough magic. Maybe not right away, but every time.

Paddling with her thumb, she found an ID not far down the list.

"Yo, Bibi, she gonna be home tonight?"

"Yeah. No problem. Not planning to cramp her gig."

"Uh-huh. I'm a night owl anyway this side of the planet."

"Whatever you're having is fine."

"Nah. I'm not fancy. Rather hang with you guys. I'll pick up a nice bottle on the way."

"Blasty. See you then."

She put the datapad away and noticed Clarence and the collections wizard staring. "Fuck's sake, you two. It's a kids' datapad. They expect five-year-olds to use it. But go ahead and perpetuate your codependent bullshit."

Tiffany departed, confident that she'd be ninety heavy richer once the bozo squad crossed their eyes and dotted their Ts.

It had been too long since she'd seen Esper. But there was only so much Karen she could stomach in the meantime. The gushing and fawning needed Esper around to dilute it. Still, hanging out with the Richelieu household staff until Esper's campaign shit was done for the day would give her a chance to catch up on the family gossip ahead of time.

All of it *almost* made up for Jimmy Rucker dicking her around and dragging her to rescue a pair of kids who didn't need her help.

———

The *Kierkegaard* was a lived-in sort of homey, more akin to a college dormitory than a terrestrial family dwelling. Its cargo hold was packed with crate after crate of limited-edition Luna-Berri Snakki Bars and little else. The stash would have been impressive if the hold had been larger, but it was *still* more Snakki Bars than Eric intended to eat in a lifetime.

"Nice ship," he commented as Lorenzo led the way inside. The next room was a common living space with a circular layout with six reclining lounge chairs, all angled toward the pedestal of a holo-projector. A cramped spiral stairway in the corner led to a mezzanine with a see-through mesh of metal floor. Doors all around the mezzanine presented tantalizing opportunities for exploration before he remembered that there wasn't much *to* this ship. If it was as little on the inside as it was on the outside—a reasonable assumption for a science-built ship —then those doors must have led to closets.

"Don't need the sass," Lorenzo shot back as he made his way to the front of the ship.

"He's serious," Jessie called out. "We grew up on a ship not much bigger than this."

"Spacers, eh?" Figgy asked as he sprawled onto a lounger, one of just two that wasn't spilling over with clutter.

"Guess that's what they call people who grow up in the Black Ocean," Jessie countered.

Figgy gestured circles with his vaporizer. Out in the starport, it had smelled, but inside the ship, the odor of hallucinogenic smoke permeated the air. Eric couldn't place the exact blend. "Sentient creatures relate through inanities, confirming details of one another's lives even when they're obvious. Common acknowledgment builds a paradigm of intersectional understanding."

Jessie shouted ahead. "Does he come with a translator?"

Eric switched to Kejathi. "Sorry. I'd say she's not always like this, but we haven't seen a lot of each other the past few years. I suspect this is normal for her. I wouldn't take offense."

The laaku in the tracksuit blew a cloud of smoke and replied in his own language. "You seem like the kind of man who doesn't take offense even when he should."

"Are you two talking about me behind my back?" Jessie demanded.

Eric glanced her up and down. "You're facing us."

"Sit," the laaku advised. "You look like the before holo for a walk-in med center. I'll have Lorry dig out the med kit once we're astral."

The ship rumbled. Through dark-tinted windows, the starport drifted by, then fell away.

"Can you just point me to it? I can self-medicate."

"If it's just the pain..." The laaku flipped his vaporizer around and offered her a puff.

"No, thanks. No offense, but I think I need to keep my wits right now."

Figgy nodded sagely. "Trust issues."

They were being bad guests. Eric took one of the cluttered lounge seats and started folding the laundry piled thereon. "I was pretty up front that we were fugitives."

"And yet you fold laundry like a teenager, not a wizard."

Eric examined his own handiwork self-consciously. "What's wrong with my folding?"

"Those clothes are soiled."

"Oh." Eric unceremoniously dumped the pile on the floor.

Figgy cackled. "Your sister is an asshole, but you I like." Eric was ready to defend the laaku against Jessie's ire but realized that the laaku had switched back to Kejathi again.

"Hey," Jessie interrupted. "I know the word for 'asshole.'"

"Ahh. Humans," Figgy commented with a grin.

There was a tingle. Gentle. Impersonal. Like the kind of massage a buzzing chair gives. Even through the tinted glassteel, he could tell the astral outside was a boring light gray. Slow. Bland. Same as almost every other ship in the galaxy might use. While the color couldn't tell him anything, that *felt* like maybe a 2 AU drop.

They could easily take over the ship.

Jessie knew how to pilot things.

It would be much faster flying if he nudged them down into the triple digits of astral space—or however far down it went.

But this wasn't a race anymore. It was a game of hide-and-seek. Maybe a shell game.

Wherever they next set foot on a planet not aligned with Mars, he and Jessie would disappear, maybe for good.

They didn't need to hurt these nice people, and Jessie had displayed an indifference on that front that needed monitoring.

Eric decided then and there that he'd be keeping his sister's violent impulses in check.

━━

Captain Byron dropped a med kit on the bunk beside her. The quarters on the upper floor of the *Kierkegaard* were little more than a monk's cell. In fact, they were no larger than the cell she'd been kept in on Mars. But the door opened from the inside, and the mattress, while lumpy and in need of fumigation, actually prevented feeling the surface beneath it.

"You good? Because I'm no medic."

Jessie nodded. "Yeah. Nothing I haven't done before." She popped the lid on the box and took a quick visual inventory. "You guys don't use this much, huh?" She blew dust off a roll of dermal tape.

"I call that a good thing. Neither of us cooks, and I pay a real mechanic to tune us up on core worlds. Not a lot of opportunity to get hurt... as long as you don't get into bar fights."

Jessie didn't take the bait. He was angling for evidence that they weren't actually Class A fugitives. That they were frauds. That they were still trying to scam him out of this free ride he was offering.

"Hey. I never got around to asking. Where we heading?"

Byron leaned against the doorjamb. "See? That's how I can tell you're really on the run. Anyone looking for a ride *to* somewhere would have made sure, at the very least, that we weren't heading the opposite direction."

Jessie didn't have the mental bandwidth for banter. "How

about you just tell me? I'm more tired than you can possibly imagine."

"Little place called Station Echo Nine."

"Earth-aligned?"

"Nah. Not much of anything aligned. They've held off declaring for either side, so traders like me and Figgy can run cargo for both sides."

"You're not Martian?"

Byron pointed to himself. "Me? I'm just a colony kid working for the League of Independent Planets."

Jessie turned the potential acronym in her head. "LIP?"

"LoIP. I know. Awkward as hell. Don't think they really vetted the name before announcing it. It was a quick deal once the war broke out. Man, you really *are* from five years ago, aren't you?"

"How much did Eric tell you?"

"You should learn Kejathi. LoIP is using English for now, but they're considering Kejathi as the official language of diplomacy."

"What colonies joined LoIP?" Settling in neutral space sounded like a damn good idea, depending on how many of the big players decided to sit this one out.

"The non-human ones. ARGO broke up. They couldn't kick out Earth *or* Mars, so everyone else left and formed their own alliance. Phabian and Keru are the main military powers, but Meyang, Ages VI, Garrelon and New Garrelon, Poltid... pretty much everyone else. They've got enough muscle that nobody's messing with them until the civil war's settled."

"Wow..."

ARGO had collapsed. There was more to this story—obviously—but she couldn't figure out how it had all gone down. The nagging suspicion that she and Eric were responsible couldn't dig its claws in; they just weren't that important in the grand scheme.

"You said it, girl. Hell of a galaxy to show up into. Anyway, I'll be in yelling distance if you need anything."

Jessie had ideas. Unfortunately, her body was in no condition to take advantage of them. Byron was built out of the Hollyworld mold of ladies' dreams. He had a relaxed self-assurance. Best of all, he didn't come across as clingy.

Realizing the awkward pause, Jessie quickly filled it. "I gotta know. Why you keep Figgy around? He doesn't seem all that useful."

Lorenzo Byron burst out laughing. "It's *his* ship I'm captaining. He's my one and only VIP passenger. You and your brother are steerage. And yeah, Figarus of Alpsen is"—he turned and raised his voice toward the lower level—"a lazy, pretentious parking brake of a philosopher." He snickered. "It's all right. We're tight. Get yourself cleaned up and join us for some dinner."

"Thanks." Jessie resumed poking through the med kit as Byron took his leave.

But the ship's captain paused, one hand halfway to swinging the door shut. "Oh, and I noticed that look." He shot her a wink.

And he closed the door.

For a hot second, Jessie felt her cheeks flush. Then she realized he was just saving her the trouble of guessing games. It would be days to Space Station Echo Nine.

―――

A night's sleep had done a universe of good for her battered body. Jessie hadn't meant to fall asleep. But in the relative safety of a ship whose crew passed the sniff test for trustworthiness, the whirlwind since Eric's little "accident" had caught up with her.

She woke up sore, hungover with fatigue, but mentally alert.

Breakfast came via a laaku food recombinator. She ate a breakfast of completely nutritious sausage and eggs, washed down with cheap coffee. Eric had happy-face chocolate pancakes from the kiddie options.

Once they'd finished eating, Eric broached a subject Jessie had been willing to put off a while longer.

"Can we borrow a comm?"

Byron chuckled. "Hey, you're the ones lying low. I'm trusting you're not going to turn yourselves in or anything stupid."

"Our parents."

Jessie winced.

Eric's look of concern fixed on her in an instant. "You still in pain?"

"Some."

Figgy ate chocolate mousse with his lower hands, sprawled in his lounge chair. "Filial reluctance. I have the same reaction when the prospect of communicating with my own mother and father rises."

"Go ahead," Lorenzo told them. "I assume I can trust a wizard in my cockpit if he keeps his hands in his sleeves?"

"Figuratively, at least," Eric replied. "I don't have loose enough sleeves, and I don't know if I should buy any in the near future."

Jessie led the way. She squeezed through the tight quarters of a ship that may have been designed for laaku-sized crew, now that she considered it. While it met General Ergonomic Standard, the layout leaned heavily to Phabian design.

Eric plopped into the co-pilot's seat and hugged his arms to his body.

Jessie found the center console with its vid display. Considering the mess she was, a voice-only comm might have been the best course, but Mom was going to want to see them. She relented and punched in the old home code she knew by heart.

No response.

She double-checked the comm ID and tried again.

No response.

"Maybe they're playing a show," Eric suggested.

Jessie shook her head. "Mom has it forward to her personal datapad. If Dad's on stage, she should still get it, and I used the 'kid code' so she knows it's one of us. It would wake her up from a dead sleep, and she's answered from the washroom enough times that I know that won't stop her."

Mom answering the datapad from the shower was a memory she wouldn't mind having a wizard erase. And if it had occurred to her ahead of the comm, she would have opted for voice-only after all.

"Try Dad, maybe?"

Jessie rubbed her chin and considered. "No. This isn't a simple call home." She punched in another code.

"Who you comming, then?"

"Yomin." But Jessie didn't even give the comm five seconds before cutting the connection.

"That... seemed quick. That was quick, right? I'm not imagining things? I've been accused of having a poor sense of time passing—I know, I know, queue the time-traveler-without-a-compass jokes—actually, that joke would work better with a clock or a sundial. If I ever run into Sato again, I'll pass along the tip."

Jessie tuned out the nonsense and watched Byron's comm panel. The instant the comm request came in, she accepted.

"*Kid?*"

"YOMIN!" Eric exclaimed.

"*Wow. Both of you, huh? Don't hang out. I'm transmitting a new ID. Comm back if you have a secure line.*"

The comm ended.

"Earth Interstellar and whatever Mars came up with might be monitoring their comms," Jessie explained. "Yomin can get us around most of what they might try."

She accepted the new comm ID and re-entered it.

Almost instantly, Mom and Dad popped up on the screen.

"Eric! Jessie!" Mom exclaimed.

"Told you they'd be fine. We didn't raise prisoners."

They looked ten years older instead of the five that had passed. Dad had trimmed his beard collar length, but it was mostly gray. Mom had gone for a blatant tint job and a tidy braid. Wrinkles had carved up both faces.

"I'm really sorry," Eric blurted. "It's all my fault. I was just trying to show Jessie that I wasn't a total fuckup and undercut my own argument by going a hundred fifty million times farther than I meant."

"We're fine."

"Sweet pea, you don't look fine."

"Mom, I've been through worse in survival training," Jessie lied. "I just wanted to know all of you are OK. The galaxy went totally to shit while we were gone."

Dad smirked. It was hard to tell behind the bushy beard, but she knew how that beard moved so well. "If I'd known the two of you were maintaining stability in the galaxy, I'd have given you a bigger allowance."

"I'll take back pay," Eric volunteered.

"We just spoke to Yomin. Everyone else OK there?"

"There's no 'there' here anymore, sweet pea," Mom explained. "We mothballed the *Mobius*. Roddy pokes at it to keep it spaceworthy, but we're grounded by choice."

"Galaxy's a mess," Dad added, rehashing the obvious. "Our right of passage was dependent on a lot of people remembering a lot of deals and certain jurisdictional crossfires. I'm just getting too old to put up with getting boarded in every system we visit."

"We're still welcome plenty of places," Mom amended quickly. "And we're getting by just fine."

"Yeah, just only so many shows you can put on in LIP space," Dad said with a shrug. "We lean heavy on Earth nostalgia that doesn't catch much slack right now."

"I heard it was LoIP."

Dad snorted. "In their dreams. One sounds stupid; the other's unpronounceable. Guess which one they get called."

"Babe, we need to get serious. Sweeties, you need a place to hide out?"

It was certainly an offer. Mom and Dad knew people. But could they really justify dragging this trouble back home? "We'll consider it. But you guys are probably going to get contacted by every agency assembled from alphabet blocks. If you haven't already, that is."

"Don't worry about us. We've got experience dealing with nosy governments."

"If you two need anything at all, just say the word."

"We've already arranged transport. We'll hop around until we find someplace that feels like we can lie low."

A laaku voice came in the background of the comm. "Hey, that them?"

"Hi, Uncle Roddy!" Eric exclaimed with a wave.

Jessie waved in a manner that hurt her ribs the least. "Hi, Roddy. Hey, is Ozzy there?"

"He's a freshman at New Garrelon Interplanetary. Galaxy's bound and determined one of my kids end up respectable." Dad made it sarcastic, but he was clearly proud.

"Oh, hey, is Uncle Enzio around?" Eric asked, his countenance the dictionary definition of eagerness.

Mom and Dad's faces fell in unison. In the background, Roddy slunk away.

"Kids... I have some bad news for you. Uncle Enzio passed on a few years ago."

A cold lump formed in Jessie's stomach. But beside her, Eric's eyes welled with tears.

"No!"

"How'd it happen?" Jessie inquired, trying to keep grounded. She hadn't even really *liked* Uncle Enzio, and he wasn't blood family. But he *was* family, and it struck a blow to childhood memories of happy times. And she absolutely *was not* going to lose her shit over him on a comm with her parents.

Dad turned on Story Mode. "He was on Earth when the rebellion broke out. There had been inquests about... well... that thing that happened. Enzio got recalled to Earth to answer a bunch of questions. Shit dragged on. And he was in Boston when the Fracture hit."

"Fracture?"

"Whatever you want to call it. The day the Convocation decided it didn't give a fuck anymore and just took over. Loyalists and traditionalists. Earthlings, Martians, colonists. Wizards drew up sides, and they didn't color inside the lines that carefully. Lotta people died. Some probably even deserved it."

"Uncle Enzio didn't!" Eric protested, crying unashamedly in the co-pilot's seat.

"Sweetie, I'm sorry," Mom said in that voice that made so many problems melt away. But not this one. "There's nothing you could have done. It's politics. Wizard politics. Just find a place to lie low and stay safe."

"We will," Jessie promised.

"Kiddos, I got more bad news. Yomin says we shouldn't keep this comm open. Just in case. She's transmitting you a new code to use next time you need to talk. Just stick together. I know you two can do anything if you plan it out. After all, you're *my* kids."

Despite the grim turn the comm had taken, Jessie snickered. "Sure, Dad. Love you both."

"Love you," Mom and Dad replied in unison.

Eric said nothing. He was too deep in his sobs. The comm went dark.

"I'm so sorry. I know he meant a lot to you."

Eric took a deep breath between sobs. "He was on Earth because of *me*! I got Uncle Enzio killed!" Then, he took another shuddering breath and composed himself. "No. I got ARGO killed."

"Huh? How can that possibly be your fault?"

"Uncle Enzio was Mordecai The—"

"Don't start with that shit again. Show a little respect. Mourn the man; don't turn him into something he's not."

Eric rubbed his eyes. "I don't know why, but it makes me feel better. It shouldn't. Because Mordecai The Brown died once before, and this time, I'm worried he did it again."

"You think he got away somehow?" Jessie asked skeptically.

For one of the few times she could remember, Eric looked her squarely in the eye.

"No. I'm worried Uncle Enzio conquered Earth."

****

Ready for more *Black Ocean: Passage of Time?*
Grab Mission 2, Terran Incognito

BOOKS BY J. S. MORIN

Black Ocean

Black Ocean is a vivid 26th century story universe where science and magic coexist—sort of.

Black Ocean: Galaxy Outlaws

Black Ocean: Galaxy Outlaws is a fast-paced fantasy space opera series about the small crew of the *Mobius* trying to squeeze out a living. If you love fantasy and sci-fi, and still lament over the cancellation of *Firefly*, *Black Ocean: Galaxy Outlaws* is the series for you.

Read about the *Black Ocean: Galaxy Outlaws* series and discover where to buy at: galaxyoutlawsmissions.com

Black Ocean: Astral Prime

Co-written with author M.A. Larkin, *Black Ocean: Astral Prime* hearkens back to location-based space sci-fi classics like *Babylon 5* and *Star Trek: Deep Space Nine*. *Astral Prime* builds on the rich *Black Ocean* universe, introducing a colorful cast of characters for new and returning readers alike. Come along for the ride as a minor outpost in the middle of nowhere becomes a key point of interstellar conflict.

Read about the *Black Ocean: Astral Prime* series and discover where to buy at: astralprimemissions.com

Black Ocean: Mercy for Hire

Black Ocean: Mercy for Hire follows the exploits of a pair of do-gooder bounty hunters who care more about saving the day than securing a payday. The series builds on the rich *Black Ocean* universe, centering on a couple of fan-favorites and introducing a colorful cast for new and returning readers alike. Fans of vigilante justice and heroes who exemplify the word will love this series.

Read about *Black Ocean: Mercy for Hire* and discover where to buy at: mercyforhiremissions.com

Black Ocean: Mirth & Mayhem

Black Ocean: Mirth & Mayhem delves into the origins of two vagabonds making their living among the stars. Mort is a wizard coming to grips with a life on the run and estrangement from the comforts and respect he had on Earth. Brad is an impressionable youth, too clever for his—or anyone's—good. And Chuck Ramsey is the mold that Brad's trying to break out of, which is harder than he could ever have dreamed.

Read about *Black Ocean: Mirth & Mayhem* and discover where to buy at: mirthandmayhemmissions.com

Black Ocean: Passage of Time

The year was 2586. A few minutes later, it was 2591. Caught up in a time travel snafu, Eric and Jessie Ramsey become fugitives from the people who want answers as to how they did it—and where their loyalties lie in the galactic war that broke out in their absence.

Read about *Black Ocean: Passage of Time* and discover where to buy at: passageoftimemissions.com

Twinborn Chronicles

The *Twinborn Chronicles* is an epic fantasy saga based on the possibility that our dreams offer us a glimpse into the life of another – another who can get the same glimpse into our world. Read about the *Twinborn Chronicles* and discover where to buy at: twinbornchronicles.com

Twinborn Chronicles: Awakening

Experience the journey of mundane scribe Kyrus Hinterdale who discovers what it means to be Twinborn—and the dangers of getting caught using magic in a world that thinks it exists only in children's stories.

Twinborn Chronicles: War of 3 Worlds

Then continue on into the world of Korr, where the Mad Tinker and his daughter try to save the humans from the oppressive race of Kuduks. When their war spills over into both Tellurak and Veydrus, what alliances will they need to forge to make sure the right side wins?

Project Transhuman

Project Transhuman brings genetic engineering into a post-apocalyptic Earth, 1000 years aliens obliterated all life.

These days, even the humans are built by robots.

Charlie7 is the oldest robot alive. He's seen everything from the fall of mankind at the hands of alien invaders to the rebuilding of a living world from the algae up. But what he hasn't seen in over a thousand years is a healthy, intelligent human. When Eve stumbles into his life, the old robot finally has something worth coming out of retirement for: someone to protect.

Read about all of the *Project Transhuman* books and discover where to buy at: projecttranshuman.com

Sins of Angels

Co-written with author M.A. Larkin, *Sins of Angels* is an epic space opera series set 3000 years after the fall of Earth. With the scope of *Dune* and the adventurous spirit of *Indiana Jones*, it delivers a conflict that spans galaxies and rests on the spirit of brave researcher Professor Rachel Jordan. Follow the complete saga, and watch as the fate of our species hangs in the balance.

Read about *Sins of Angels* and discover where to buy at: sinsofangelsbooks.com

Shadowblood Heir

Shadowblood Heir explores what would happen if the writer of your favorite epic fantasy TV show died before the show ended—and the show was responsible. If you wonder what it would be like if an epic fantasy world invaded our world, this urban fantasy story might give you that glimpse.

Read about *Shadowblood Heir* and discover where to buy at: shadowbloodheir.com

EMAIL INSIDERS

You made it to the end! Maybe you're just persistent, but hopefully that means you enjoyed the book. But this is just the end of one story. If you'd like reading my books, there are always more on the way!

Perks of being an Email Insider include:

- Notification of book releases (often with discounts)
- Inside track on beta reading
- Advance review copies (ARCs)
- Access to Inside Exclusive bonus extras and giveaways
- Best of my blog about fantasy, science fiction, and the art of worldbuilding

Sign up for the my Email Insiders list at: jsmorin.com/updates

ABOUT THE AUTHOR

I am a creator of worlds and a destroyer of words. As a fantasy writer, my works range from traditional epics to futuristic fantasy with starships. I have worked as an unpaid Little League pitcher, a cashier, a student library aide, a factory grunt, a cubicle drone, and an engineer—there is some overlap in the last two.

Through it all, though, I was always a storyteller. Eventually I started writing books based on the stray stories in my head, and people kept telling me to write more of them. Now, that's all I do for a living.

I enjoy strategy, worldbuilding, and the fantasy author's privilege to make up words. I am a gamer, a joker, and a thinker of sideways thoughts. But I don't dance, can't sing, and my best artistic efforts fall short of your average notebook doodle. When you read my books, you are seeing me at my best.

My ultimate goal is to be both clever and right at the same time. I have it on good authority that I have yet to achieve it.

Connect with me online
jsmorin.com

facebook.com/authorjsmorin

twitter.com/authorjsmorin

bookbub.com/authors/j-s-morin

goodreads.com/JSMorin

tiktok.com/@authorjsmorin

www.ingramcontent.com/pod-product-compliance
Lightning Source LLC
Chambersburg PA
CBHW032015240626
47153CB00003B/1253